SLIPPING INTO DARKNESS

D. M. BOURGEOIS

Publisher's Note: This is a work of fiction. Names, characters, places, and incidents are a product of the author's imagination. Locales and public names are sometimes used for atmospheric purposes. Any resemblance to actual people, living or dead, or to businesses, companies, events, institutions, or locales is completely coincidental.

Book Cover Design by ebooklaunch.com
Book Layout © 2017 BookDesignTemplates.com
Edited by Brandy Delgado brandywood1@gmail.com

Slipping Into Darkness/ D. M. Bourgeois-- 1st ed.
ISBN 978-1-7357823-0-0

SLIPPING INTO DARKNESS

This book is dedicated to my family and friends. Thanks for encouraging me to pursue my dream and for being patient with me as I fumbled my way through it.

I would like to acknowledge a few people that read my work and gave me critical feedback. My incredible husband Glenn, my stepmom Gilda Bourgeois, my brother Danny Bourgeois, my grandson Davin Ortego, and my good friends Charisse Zanca and Jacob Zanca.

A special thank you to my dear friend Charisse Zanca. I don't think I could have published this book without you. Your encouragement and support mean the world to me.

To my husband Glenn. Since the day we met you've tried to make all my dreams come true. I thank you for your love and support because without you none of this would matter.

Most importantly, I want to thank God for all the Blessings in my life and for giving me the wisdom to know that through him all things are possible.

CHAPTER 1

SEPTEMBER 2017 PRESENT DAY

Abby looked back but only for a quick glance. *Run! Abby run!* It was dark and difficult to see clearly. Staying on the trail had proved to be too dangerous, so she looked around for someplace to hide, but where? Adrenaline pumping, Abby pushed herself to a new level. At every step forward, her body was shocked with pain and she felt as if she were running in slow motion. The brush was so thick, and she faced obstacles at every turn. She ducked behind a tree to regroup. She felt the early morning dew drop from the trees and jumped as it contacted her skin. *Get a grip Abby. Think! Where is Griff? He was right by my side now he's gone. And what was that thing chasing me?*

Abby stood up with the help of her walking stick. She peeked from behind the tree and was finding it difficult to identify what was coming towards her. It appeared to be a black bear but there are no bears there. She knew she couldn't out-run the bear and instead stood paralyzed with fear. He was so close now that she could hear every breath he took. Her heart was beating so fast that Abby was sure the loud pounding sound would disclose her location. Bracing herself against the tree for support, she stepped out and swung the stick as hard as she could. All she saw was the stick connecting with black fur that turned red. She took off running again and this time didn't look back.

Abby woke screaming as she looked around the room confused trying to figure out where she was. Griff jumped out of bed from a dead sleep and ran to her side.

"Abby, what's wrong? What happened? Are you okay?"

She didn't move for a moment, as she tried to make sense of what happened. "I think I was dreaming. I've been having these odd dreams the last few nights and in every one of them, I have an old walking stick that I take with me on my walks. It's funny, I can't seem to recall anything about the dreams except the need for a walking stick. I believe something is telling me to get a stick, but I'm not sure why. I probably could use one because just this morning, during my morning walk, several deer ran across my path, and scared the heck out of me. They came out of nowhere! You never know what I'll encounter out there, so I would feel safer if I had something that I could defend myself with. Besides, I can use all the help I can get, considering the shape I'm in. Running from something dangerous wouldn't end well. I think I need to find a walking stick; something old and unusual, unique. Can we go to Summit for lunch today?"

Griff sighed his usual sigh.

Abby Stewart, Griff's wife, was 55 years old and had been trying to get in shape for years. Every Monday started out with a new diet and an exercise plan.

Inevitably, something always came up to disrupt the plan. "Disrupt" was a nice word that described her lack of discipline because she could never seem to stick with it. Being from New Orleans, every social event was centered on food. It didn't matter the event; everyone brought a dish. That had always been a way of life for Abby, and it would be a hard habit to break.

He gave her a brisk nod.

Summit, Mississippi's crowds this time of the day weren't so bad. Usually, the mobs were heavier in the late afternoon and on weekends. Anyway, Tuesdays were usually slow and quite peaceful. Griff was so busy lately; a quiet lunch was exactly what he was looking for.

"Let's roll," he said.

Summit was a quaint little town in southern Mississippi. Beautiful trees lined both sides of Main Street and there were several antique shops and good restaurants to lure in tourist. The temperature could get rather humid in the summertime, but in September, it was quite pleasant. While the days were nice, the nights were spectacular. Being away from the city, the stars illuminated the sky like a million little lightning bugs. The way they blanketed the sky created a feeling of security. It reminded a lot of folks of a simpler time. Things were moving way too fast these days and it sure was nice to slow it down every once in a while. Griff and Abby smiled at one another as they pulled into an open parking lot, under an oak tree in the middle of Summit, ready to enjoy lunch and some shopping, without any indication of the evil that was to come.

They browsed in a few different places but were unable to find the kind of walking stick Abby was looking for. A few stores sold them by bulk, but there was nothing unique about that. Besides, Abby could find that in the stores where she lived in Crown Point. It was amazing just to walk through the touristy shops, full of antiques filling each room. The merchandise was arranged in a way that took you back in time. Some rooms were set up like an actual bedroom from the early fifties, with the décor to match. An old lamp sat on a nightstand with an old-time alarm clock next to it. It would be interesting to know if all the stuff in one room came from the same person, or if they just set it up piece by piece, as each item was acquired. Most of the stuff looked like it had been in there a long time and was probably worthless, but if you were lucky, you might find exactly what you were looking for.

After shopping for an hour or so, Griff and Abby decided to grab lunch. There were several little cafés to choose from, so Abby let Griff decide. Of course, for him, a good homemade hamburger and a tall glass of sweet tea always hit the spot.

There was a perfect little café on the corner that caught Griff's attention. Nostalgia kicked in immediately and they felt like they had gone back in time and had stepped into an old-time malt shop. There was counter seating inside and tables set up for outside dining. It reminded them of K&B Drugstore. There was a vintage jukebox in the far corner playing Patsy Cline and advertisements of Malts and Root beer Floats on the wall behind the counter. They both felt transformed to a time long ago, and they loved it. They placed their orders before deciding to settle at one of the tables outside.

"Will we ever be able to find the kind of walking stick I'm looking for? I can't believe we haven't found one yet."

Griff mused, "Patience was never one of your strong suits. We just started looking today. Give it some time and I'm sure you will find exactly what you are looking for."

Abby sighed.

Griff was right. She was not very patient. But it was so frustrating when you know exactly what you were looking for and couldn't find it. It seemed to Abby that antique stores in a small town like Summit would have all sorts of different walking sticks. There were still a few stores to check after lunch, so she remained hopeful that she would find one today.

After lunch, they headed back down Main Street. The next store they walked into was called "Second Chances." Abby went straight to the checkout and asked if they had any old walking sticks. By now, she knew Griff was done with shopping for the day and she didn't want to waste any more time. They showed her a barrel full of brand-new ones.

Disappointed, she motioned to Griff to go. Just as they were walking out, an old woman came from the far side of the store, and in her hand was the exact walking stick Abby had seen in her dreams.

Abby perked up, "That's it! That's exactly what I'm looking for."

At that, Griff turned around and saw the stick for the first time. While Abby was thrilled, Griff was struck with an odd feeling, sending his heart racing. It came on so quickly and subtle, that he wasn't quite sure what to make out of it. Since he was ready to get home and he saw Abby's excitement, he managed to brush it off, and asked, "Can we go home now?"

"Yes, let me check out and I'll meet you back at the car."

As she picked up the stick, the checkout lady looked a little confused.

"Where did you find this one? I haven't seen it before, and it doesn't have a price tag."

"One of your sales ladies just brought it to me from over there," Abby said, pointing to the other side of the store. As quickly as it came, all concern lifted from her face and the clerk rang up the stick and wished Abby a good day. Abby left the store.

She found Griff waiting by the car. With the joy of having found what she was looking for, Abby struck up conversation and laughter during the ride home, and upon arrival, they both settled in for a quiet afternoon nap. Abby smiled thinking, *What a successful afternoon*, not realizing that it would be that afternoon that would reset the course of her life as she knew it, and from that day forward, things would never be the same.

CHAPTER 2

The next morning turned out to be a beautiful morning for a walk. Even though it was fall in Crown Point, the afternoons were still quite hot. This year, the fall whether never seemed to arrive. Normally, by this time of year, the high was about 80, which was still hot, but yesterday it reached 89. Griff didn't mind the heat; in fact, he preferred it. That was the thing he and Abby disagreed about the most. Abby's countless hot flashes seemed to be a constant state of being. After beating cancer, she was prescribed Tamoxifen, a hormone blocker. Just when it seemed like she would actually survive menopause, the new meds threw her right back into it, making the hot afternoons almost unbearable. She's counting the days until she can stop taking it. But for now, she and Griff battle with the air conditioner, daily. She often daydreamed, *If only he could have just one hot flash, he would be much more sympathetic.*

"With this heat I'll have to get up extra early if I want to stay on track." Abby was frustrated. It had become a ritual for her to walk several miles every morning before breakfast. Sometimes, Griff joined her, but more often than not, he was already off to work at the shop before she woke up. Although he was supposed to retire a while back, he still spent a lot of time there. She thought he was prolonging it because he stilled enjoyed working and was worried about having 'nothing to do'. He had commented more than once that a lot of people retire and then fall ill, or worse. He probably had to take it a little at a time and become comfortable with his decision. When he finally did fully retire, it would be a life changer for both of them.

Abby didn't mind walking alone. There was something about just absorbing nature that kept her company enough. The nature and the alone time allowed her to keep her mind clear. Further, she saw it as a time to reflect on life: past, present, and future. She also enjoyed that time with prayer. She and Griff considered themselves devout Christians and believed that prayer was everything.

On this particular morning, Griff was home and decided to join in the walk. The air was crisp which made for an easier workout. Sometimes the humidity was so thick it was hard to breathe.

"Hopefully, this week I'll have time to work on the treadmill; it's just been so crazy lately I'm exhausted when I get home." Griff knew his wife understood but also knew she was eager to get back to using the treadmill for exercising instead of a clothes rack. Abby had been asking him to fix it for months now and he could tell she was beginning to get a little impatient with him.

"I hope so. I really want to continue my exercise, but I can't take this heat."

"I see you're getting some use out of that old walking stick. It's a little tall for you. Do you want me to shorten it?" Griff was always looking around to see what needed to be fixed.

"Absolutely not! I really like that it's old and full of history. Imagine all the people who have used this stick, the places it has been. I wish there was a way to find out exactly where it's been. I bet if it could talk it would have a lot to say, and probably not all good."

"I'm sure you're right. The thing looks pretty old and worn. I'm surprised it's in such good shape. It must be solid. By the way, did the clerk at the store happen to give you any history on the stick? Sometimes the people who drop off stuff to be sold at the store share a little history."

"She didn't say anything. We were in a hurry, and I didn't take the time to ask. I was just so excited to finally find it. I know it's kind of silly to care about something like this, but it just adds a little extra joy to my walk."

They continued to walk and enjoy the beautiful scenery. Ideally, they tried to walk about an hour. That didn't always happen, but today it looked like it would.

"On a different note, how are things with E.R? Can you believe we have a grandson graduating from high school this year? It seems like yesterday we were at the camp, and he was five?"

Evan Robert, E.R. for short, was their only grandson. Griff and Abby were blessed with two daughters, Alex, and Harper, who were seventeen years apart. Alex, their oldest, and her husband Finn had two children, E.R. who was seventeen and Gabrielle, who was 10. Abby recalled the conversation she had about E.R. with her daughter Alex, yesterday.

"He's doing okay. He has a lot going on with school and sports. Alex is hoping he gets into the Engineering program at the University of New Orleans. After visiting several schools, he decided to only apply there, hoping he can stay close to home, which makes me happy, because I miss him already. It's an adjustment not seeing him like we used to. But we have to let him grow up. I just hope he doesn't want us to start calling him Evan Robert instead of E.R. like we've always done. That's where I draw the line." Abby smiled as she thought of E.R. as a child.

"Is it really that difficult to get into the program?" Griff asked. "I know he has the grades but what else does it go by?"

"Not sure. I just know Alex is doing all she can to help ensure he has the best chance. She and Finn have really encouraged and supported their son and I know he will be fine however it turns out. Unfortunately, the campus apartments were already full by the time he decided to apply. I wish he could've stayed there at least for the first semester so he could really get the college experience."

Understanding that E.R. was the light of Abby's world, Griff knew she would not sit back and wait for the outcome. She had never been good at waiting and without a doubt; she would do everything possible to ensure that whatever her grandson wanted would happen. "Well, what will be will be," Griff whispered to Abby.

They had walked for close to an hour now. The sun was really beating down, and the air became thick. The path they walked was a combination of rock and dirt roads. By the time they were finished, they were both drenched and ready to jump into a cool shower before their day began. Living in the south, like most places, had its own unique qualities, some good and some bad. That time of year, Hurricanes were the big concern, and that included the prospect of having to evacuate at a moment's notice. But the weather was beautiful year-round, notwithstanding July and August. The winters there are mild and usually short. They got their fair share of cold weather; in fact, it snowed the past few years. They could use a little colder winter to kill off the mosquito population.

That had to be the worst part of living in the south, mosquitoes, and the number one complaint. Without cold winters to kill them off, it was almost impossible to enjoy the evenings without either a screen or a lot of bug spray. Luckily, Abby had a screened in patio at her house.

Most of the time, you could find someone sitting out there enjoying the evening. Unfortunately, it was a constant chore to keep the patio clean. Today, Abby decided to tackle it before she went to meet her best friend Olivia for lunch. Earlier, she received a call from Olivia and was asked if they could meet. She sounded a little upset, so Abby agreed and decided she would just have to do what she could with the patio.

Abby and Olivia had been friends since grade school. They raised their children together. Now that the children were grown, they hoped to spend more time together. Anytime she needed Olivia, she was always there no matter what. Abby would never forget that despite overwhelming support from friends and family, in 2014, when she was battling breast cancer, it was Olivia who was there every day. She was her morning call of encouragement and her nightly call to make sure she was okay. She was a bright light in the darkness. Griff was also there every step of the way and Abby could not have endured half of it without him. But it was somehow just a different kind of support; a girl needs her best friend.

Before she headed out to meet Olivia, concern bubbled up again because she seemed a little down the last time they spoke. Since Olivia's last child left for college, things at home had been a little strained. Abby thought she was probably struggling with empty nest syndrome. She and Griff never did go through that. They loved their children more than life itself, but they both felt like it was an accomplishment that their children grew up and were able to be independent. As long as their children were happy, they were happy. Plus, they loved having time to spend together again, just the two of them. They were enjoying every moment of life. Griff always said, "If I died tomorrow, I would have no regrets. I have lived my life to the fullest. There are no 'What if's'ever."

Especially with his diagnoses of prostate cancer earlier that year, they had learned to live every day as though it was their last. They thanked God every day for the blessings they had received. Like Abby's earlier diagnosis, Griff came through his remarkably well. He was only down a few days. He attributes his quick recovery to the spinning class he attended three times a week. Whatever the reason, they were grateful for their blessings.

It was almost 11:30am now, and time to finish up the patio and get ready for lunch. They were meeting at Abby's favorite place, a restaurant called Gattuso's in Old Gretna. It was a local place that served really good food and provided a pleasant atmosphere for their customers. They usually met there at least once a week; sometimes more. Lately, they had both been so busy that they were lucky to squeeze in any time together. Abby made a mental note to always make time for the important things. She realized that things change quickly in this world, and that it was important to cherish every moment.

Gattuso's looked a little crowded. She forgot it was Thursday, five-dollar burger day. Abby arrived a little early, so she decided to walk down the street to a few of the shops. The weather was nice out today and Olivia was always late. Abby shopped for about 20 minutes, and then decided to go get a table. As she was about to cross the street, she noticed an old car parked a few cars away. Thanks to her husband's interest in old cars, she recognized it as an old Dodge Dart. There was an elderly man sitting behind the wheel and he seemed to be staring at her. Doubtful that was the case, Abby looked away. He was probably just there to meet someone or possibly waiting on his wife. Often, Griff dropped Abby off when it was crowded so she didn't have to find a place to park. A little unnerved, Abby headed back to the restaurant to meet Olivia.

CHAPTER 3

A few years back Gattuso's expanded the restaurant to include outdoor seating, but Abby thought again how full it was today. Gattuso's had daily specials and featured bands on weekends. It was nice to have someplace local to enjoy good food and music. New Orleans was known for both and while she and Griff enjoyed the French Quarter, sometimes they liked to stay close to home. Since they lived on the Westbank side of the Mississippi River, going over the river, in and out of the city usually meant hours of bumper-to-bumper traffic.

Abby decided to sit outside so they could enjoy the mild afternoon. Also, inside the restaurant was usually pretty noisy, and since she and Olivia were meeting to talk, she thought sitting outside would be less distracting. While waiting to be seated, she saw several people she knew. The hostess herself was her niece Eliza's sister-n-law. Her niece used to work there before she got married. They engaged in casual conversation about the weather and the upcoming holidays.

"How have you been Anna? I see you're busy today."

"I'm doing alright. I've just been busy with school and work. It's been nonstop all day. I can't wait for the holiday break," Anna looked around for a table. "How many are with you today?"

"Just two of us and we'd like to sit outside if you have an open table. It's such a beautiful day and not as loud as inside."

Olivia was late, of course. Abby enjoyed her time sitting outside and 'people watching.' That was something Griff introduced her to years ago. At every opportunity, he would find a little café on a main street and enjoy watching how different everyone could be. He would try to guess what they did for a living or where they were from. Now, Abby found herself doing the same thing. Suddenly, she noticed the time and began to worry. Olivia was always late, but not this late. Just as Abby went for her phone to give Olivia a ring, she saw her drive up and park.

Olivia looked tired and not at all like herself. Normally, she had a bubbly personality, which felt like a ray of sunshine when she entered a room. Her presence demanded your attention. With her long black hair usually curled and full of life and her eyes as blue as the sea, she was an attractive woman. She was very slender for her 5'8" height and had beautiful glossy skin. People always migrate to positive, upbeat people. That described Olivia perfectly, with her infectious smile and her gleeful childish laugh; everyone flocked to her. Abby thought, *One of the reasons we've been friends for so long was because we are a lot alike*. They try to make the best out of any situation and could always lean on one another when life got too overwhelming. Today, it was Abby's turn to do the uplifting. With the hint of wrinkles over Olivia's forehead and the dark circles under her eyes, it seemed she has her work cut out for her. Clearly, Olivia was dealing with something stressful, but they usually talked most every day, so Abby couldn't imagine what it could be. Whatever it was, they would get through it together, just as they always did.

She stood to greet Olivia. "I'm over here."

Making her way through the crowded patio, Olivia walked up to Abby and gave her a hug, as she always did. Normally, she fluttered like a butterfly when she entered a space, smiling at people and stopping to greet those around her. Today, she just walked straight towards Abby with her gaze fixed.

"I hope you don't mind I choose an outside table. When you called and said you needed to talk, I thought that out here would be best."

"It's perfect. Did you order anything yet because I need a drink? It's been a rough few days."

Concerned, Abby answered, "Not yet. I just sat down. They have specials and drinks listed on that flyer. Let's order because you're beginning to scare me. I know something's going on and I can't believe you have only now called me to talk. Please tell me everyone's okay."

She shrugged her shoulders, "The kids are fine. Jack's fine. He just found out that he's being transferred to Texas! I can't move to Texas! My life is here! My kids are here! My friends are here! You're here!" Olivia began to tear up and could barely talk. "Since the oil spill in 2010, his company has been losing work. They finally decided to shut the Louisiana branch down and offered Jack a job at the main branch in Houston. I know I should be grateful that he still has a job, but I can't help feeling like this move would be a mistake. He just found out a few days ago and I've been sick ever since."

"Oh my God Olivia, why didn't you call me? I can't believe it. How does Jack feel about it?"

Olivia rolled her eyes, "He thinks it might be an exciting new adventure for us. I know he must be a little apprehensive himself but, he's not showing it. He's probably trying to be brave for me. It's not like we have a lot of choices here. He still has several years before he retires, but at the same time, he's too old to start something new. And I don't want him to have to do that, but Abby I can't move! What am I going to do?"

Abby fired off more questions, "Is this a done deal? How much time do you have? Do you have a specific date yet? Oh Olivia, I'm sorry for all the questions but, this is very disturbing news. I completely understand why you're so upset."

"Yes, it's definite. His only choice is to transfer or be laid off. They wanted him to be there before Christmas but, thankfully, he talked them into waiting until the first of the year," she complained. Again, she was tearing up, but it looked like she felt some relief after being able to talk about it.

"That's only a few months away." Upset, Abby decided she also needed a drink. "Let's order. Now I need a drink. I'm sure everything will work out like it supposed to, but I'm with you, you can't move."

Just then, as Abby motioned for a server, the Dodge Dart she saw when she arrived earlier caught her eye, still parked down the street. The table they were sitting at had a perfect view of the main street. She wondered if it was something she should mention to Olivia or if she was being paranoid. If the man in the driver's seat was waiting on someone, he'd been waiting a long time. Griff would never wait that long for her. Feeling a tinge of anxiety, she guessed it was possible that he was sitting there so he could keep his eye on someone. She could see that he was an elderly man, maybe mid 70's, with dark hair. His body language didn't seem like he was trying to hide, making it clear he didn't care who saw him lurking. Pushing it out of her head, Abby determined she wasn't in any danger, but something about him felt creepy. It was probably all those scary movies she loved watching that had her reading too much into the situation. If that were the case, it wouldn't have been the first time. With that, Abby dismissed her suspicions and turned her focus back to the more pressing issue of losing her best friend. They ordered their food and after deciding to really enjoy their lunch, also ordered themselves a couple of drinks. Abby knew they'd have to accept the inevitable, but today they committed to enjoying the time they had left. She had never considered life without her best friend and couldn't stand the thought of it. After lunch, they parted ways, promising to keep in close touch, and see each other as much as they could before Olivia's move.

Later that day, Abby, still upset about the news Olivia delivered earlier, decided to take an afternoon walk. She needed to wrap her head around such a big change. The thought of life without her best friend scared the heck out of her. She usually felt more relaxed after a walk and figured that was what she needed to help her ease into accepting the news. On the way out the door she remembered to grab the walking stick. After buying it a few weeks before, she had forgotten it several times, and was usually too far down the walking path to turn around and get it. It not only made her feel a little protected, but she found that it helped with the more difficult stretch of her walk where the road was a little steeper.

Her mind raced as she contemplated Olivia's dilemma. It seemed like they had no options, no good ones anyway. *I know Olivia said Jack didn't want to start over but, wasn't going to a new state starting over? And Houston was not that far away, maybe Jack could commute or just stay there during the week and come home on weekends. Olivia could move in with us and use our spare bedroom.* Abby continued to toss idea after idea as she frantically searched for a solution.

A cool front came through in the afternoon, which made the evening quite pleasant. *Of course, it could be 40 degrees outside, and I would still be sweating,* Abby thought feeling frustrated. That seemed to be life these days. She had been walking for about thirty minutes and still felt agitated and on edge. She didn't like this out of control feeling and this situation had her feeling out of control. Frustrated, she picked up the pace, hoping her walk would wear her out, which would probably be the only thing that would let her sleep that night.

As she continued to walk, Abby contemplated, *Why is this happening now? Our kids are grown, and we had so many plans for the future.* Abby always knew things would change as they got older but figured Olivia would be the constant. *Now what am I going to do? Who will I get to do all the crazy, spontaneous things I like to do?* Olivia was right there with her planning and putting into motion all their great ideas. It didn't matter what she came up with, Olivia was always game.

Abby started reminiscing about the time they had planned a murder mystery costume party that they wrote themselves. They had "name that tune" parties and "minute to win it" game nights. They did karaoke nights and planned themed Christmas parties every year. They started a scrapbook club, which they planned many themed conventions. When their daughters went to high school, they joined the parents club and planned and executed all the dances and events. They planned all their children's birthday parties together. Abby couldn't remember a time when she wasn't there. All of her memories included Olivia.

As she approached the end of her walk, she was still terribly upset. *Something has to happen. Maybe things will pick up at Jack's company. They still have a little time for things to change.* She wasn't sure how, but she decided she was going to work this out. Losing her best friend was not an option.

She had defrosted some frozen gumbo she had made a few weeks ago and had dinner ready when Griff walked in around 5pm from work. Sometimes he liked to watch the evening news and doze off a bit, but not today. She was too worked up and needed to talk to her other best friend, Griff, about what she learned today. He listened to her ramble on and on about Olivia and Jack's news. He knew this was going to be extremely hard on Abby.

Through the years, she'd had a lot of what Griff called "NBF's," new best friends. He teased her all the time because almost everyone she met became her good friend. One thing he was sure about was that it didn't matter how many friends she had, Olivia had always been her true best friend. In addition to him, Olivia was the one Abby confided in. She was the one she told her darkest and most embarrassing secrets to. Some days, Griff thought she might even prefer her over him. He knew that was not true, but he often teased her about it. Griff knew, in the Stewart household, things would be stressful for the next few months. His wife would not stop until she had exhausted all her options and helping Olivia would be her main priority. He just hoped to be able to comfort her when the time came to finally accept what was bound to happen: a long-distance relationship with her best friend.

CHAPTER 4

1967

It was reported that two people were dead, and one critically injured in a bizarre turn of events. Apparently, a quarrel broke out between three men, and it ended with two of them beaten to death. The survivor, a 75-year-old male was at the hospital in critical condition. The crime occurred at the elderly man's home in Brookhaven, Mississippi. It was not yet apparent whether the survivor was responsible for the two other deaths or was a victim himself. There were no witnesses, but people who know the homeowner said he had been acting strange lately. He lost his wife about six months ago and a few days later he had a stroke. Family members said he was doing well and just this past month, after months of rehabilitation, he was out of his wheelchair and walking with a cane. Detective Clay Hawkins from the Brookhaven Police Department said, "The details are still unclear and under investigation."

CHAPTER 5

2017

Olivia's news still had Abby on edge and as she looked for the silver lining, she took some solace in the fact that September was usually a busy time with several festivals each weekend. Staying busy was just what she needed. As a southerner, she and Griff took every opportunity to celebrate and have a party. In the month of September alone, there was the "National Fried Chicken Fest", the "Gretna Fest", the "New Orleans Irish Fest" and the list went on and on. There was a festival for just about everything. The "Gretna Fest" was a local favorite. When it started, it was one of the smaller festivals, but had since grown into a major festival, not quite on par with the annual New Orleans Jazz & Heritage Fest, but large in its own right. The Gretna Festival, which is held in late September, usually had beautiful weather, and was easily accessible. It occupied several blocks of Gretna, with street after street of all the different food vendors you could ever imagine.

The festival sets up several stages and always featured some big-name musicians. Last year, Griff and Abby saw Lynyrd Skynyrd, LeAnn Rimes, Kool & the Gang and Melissa Etheridge. Previous years' the lineup included Kid Rock, Hank Williams Jr., ZZ Top, and Greg Allman. The festival was usually the last weekend in September or the first weekend in October. The three-day festival was reasonably priced, and often became crowded at night, so people brought their chairs or sat on the levee along the Mississippi River. It was a perfect time to sit back and relax or catch up with old friends.

This year, Alex and the kids decided to go with Abby and Griff. Their daughter was always a bit of a home body, and rarely went to these events. Abby thought it would be a nice distraction for everyone. Since the festival was coming up next weekend, Abby wanted to get the patio cleaned the weekend before, so they could enjoy the Gretna Fest. That meant that this weekend would be full of working outside. They had always loved their peaceful little town, Crown Point, and they didn't mind taking care of their three-acre home, which offered just enough privacy, even if it did require quite a bit of work. Abby and Griff both really liked their neighbors and had several close friends who lived nearby. Their country life was just 30 minutes from the city, which allowed them to enjoy both busy city and peaceful living, which suited them well. Abby had just begun her work on the patio when the phone rang. She raced to get to the phone, but by the time she picked it up, the person calling had already hung up. She thought it was probably best to just ignore it and get back to work but something made her stop and think. She checked her caller ID and saw that it was Olivia. The phone rang again and this time she picked it up quickly.

"We may not have to move! They said things have changed and due to all the flooding in Houston last month, they may not shut this branch down." Olivia, unable to contain her excitement, was practically shouting on the other end of the line. She was talking so fast at first, Abby didn't recognize her voice, then when she realized who it was, she could hardly understand.

Baffled, Abby questioned Olivia. "Can you slow down. What are you talking about?"

Olivia went on, "Jack just called. He said he just received a call from his boss about the transfer. Houston is still under water from Hurricane Harvey and the office there is inoperable. They may have to find a new location for that branch and so they are rethinking the closing of this branch. This is amazing news. We don't understand what happened because when they made this decision, they already knew Houston was flooded. They had planned on moving forward anyway and that's why I think they were all in agreement for Jack to postpone his transfer until the next year. I really don't care what the reason is, I'm just so happy we might not have to move!"

"That's fantastic news Olivia. I've been so worried about this. You have no idea how relived I am. Or, maybe you do since it would've actually affected you more than me. I'm just being selfish I guess, but I've been tossing this around in my mind for days trying to find a way out for you. I've been wishing for things to stay the same. It seems like my wish has come true. This calls for a celebration."

"I'm ready for anything. What do you think we should do?"

"Well, do we want to go out with Griff and Jack, or just have a girl's night? I'm thinking maybe we should include the guys, since it does involve them. Let's go to the *Chophouse* on Magazine Street tonight and celebrate this amazing turn of events. Then next week we'll have a girl's night. Does 6pm work for you?"

"That sounds good to me. Do you want us to pick you up?"

Filled with so much emotion, Abby replied, "Yes and maybe we can catch a band somewhere after dinner. See you tonight."

Abby could not believe that was happening. She had a lot on her mind lately, but that was in the forefront ever since she met Olivia at Gattuso's that day. She was aware of the flooding in Houston; it was reported nationally and internationally. It devastated not only Houston, but Beaumont and a lot of other areas in Texas. It was reported that around August 25, Hurricane Harvey made landfall and dumped about 27 trillion gallons of water on Texas and Louisiana. It dumped nearly 50 inches of rain on Houston. It was said to be tied with Hurricane Katrina, which hit New Orleans in 2005, for being one of the costliest natural disasters.

Here we are late September, and the region is still devastated. I wonder what changed their minds about Jack's branch of the company relocating there, Abby pondered. Whatever the reason she couldn't be happier. She went back to the patio and began to work on getting things in order. Before the interruption, she had begun pressure washing the patio, which usually took a long time, but made such a difference. It always gave her a sense of peace and tranquility to sit out there. They enjoyed the patio all year round, so it's necessary to pressure wash it twice a year, since the humidity causes a green film to cover everything. Sometimes they hire someone to do it, but lately Abby had been stressed and needed something to calm her down. It was time to finish up so she can get ready for her outing with Olivia and Jack to celebrate that night. She was so excited, she had forgotten to check with Griff to confirm he was available, but she was fairly certain he was.

Jack and Olivia picked up Abby and Griff and they all headed to the city for a fun evening, after the weight had been lifted off their shoulders. With Griff and his self-entertaining sense of humor and Jack joining them, she knew they'd have a great night. While all their food was delicious, they served the best steak in the city at *Chophouse*. It melted in your mouth, and she couldn't wait. She was the type of person who ordered the same thing all the time, while Griff always tried something new every time. He liked to take his time and savor every mouthwatering bite. They often teased that he doesn't just eat he "Dines." They forgot to make reservations, but thankfully, they were seated right away.

"So, Jack, Abby told me the good news. I'm assuming that you're happy about it, I know Olivia is." Griff started off the conversation.

"I am happy about it. I know it would've been hard on Olivia. I was approaching it as a new adventure and had accepted that's what we needed to do. Now it seems things will stay the same." Jack took a sip of his drink.

"Well, we're glad you get to stay. Abby and I would've missed the time we spend with both of you. Did they give you any explanation of what changed?"

Olivia chimed in. "The office in Houston flooded last month. Supposedly, it's still inoperable."

Jack remembered he forgot to tell Olivia the rest of the news he received a little earlier. "That was a factor but with the sudden passing of Freddy Jones, the C.E.O of the company, they decided to go in a different direction."

"Wait, you didn't tell me that." Olivia, now confused, demanded, "What happened to him? Was he sick?"

"All they said was that his wife found him dead in their home last week. They just notified us today. They didn't disclose much information. It seems to be hush-hush. Everyone thought it might be suicide since he lost everything in the flood, but from what I understand, the coroner classified his death as undetermined. Who knows what happened to the poor guy? One thing's for sure, that main office is now in disarray."

Abby sat stunned for a moment. *Why does that news upset me? I don't even know the guy.* She suddenly had an overwhelming feeling that something strange was going on. It was like the feeling the main character got in a horror film just before bad things started happening. Silly, she knew, but the hair on the back of her neck seemed to stand up as Jack was telling them what happened. It looked like she was the only one with that feeling. Was she feeling guilty because she wished for something to happen? Was it a coincidence that this happened now?

Abby decided she needed to shake the unwanted feelings and turned to Olivia to ask, "What are you ordering? I think I'm going to order a steak. But first, let's get some appetizers for the table. How about we splurge and get the seafood platter appetizer? That's enough for the table and it's really good."

"That sounds great," Olivia exclaimed.

They enjoyed their meal and laughed the whole night. Griff was always good for a few laughs. He always checked out everyone in the place and tried to figure out who they looked like. Then he would say "so and so" just walked in. Then we all looked, and the resemblance was usually dead on.

Later, they decided to go to Harrah's Casino on Canal Street. That place was always busy, and on a Friday night, it was hard to find a machine to play. It always happened that the two machines they liked to play, everyone else liked to play. It was so loud in there and difficult to hold a conversation, so they decided to go to Masquerades Nightclub, which was inside Harrah's, so they could listen to the band. They enjoyed going there because it was full of people of all ages. They might be getting older, but they still loved to listen to good music and dance. Abby wouldn't say they were good dancers, but they didn't care. Especially Griff, who had always rocked a style of his own but had no rhythm at all. He definitely knew how to have fun. He seldom sat down and always ended up dancing with whoever was on the dance floor. That was what Abby loved most about him. Griff didn't care what anyone thought of him, he just enjoyed life. The nightclub was full, and they ran into a few people they knew. They even ran into people they didn't know. There was an older man who almost knocked Abby down trying to pass. He gave her a piercing look and without apologizing rushed out. Something about him seemed familiar but she didn't recognize him.

Griff and Abby danced well into the morning and when they got home, they were both exhausted. Playing back the events of the evening in her mind, Abby started to think about the strange passing of the C.E.O. at Jack's work. Feeling haunted by it, she quickly put it out of her mind and tried to focus on the things she had to do the next day. When she woke in the morning, she felt great and couldn't remember ever sleeping that well.

CHAPTER 6

The following week was uneventful and passed quickly. Abby finally finished cleaning the patio and worked on the flower bed. After the summer heat had passed, the poor plants were in bad shape. She cleaned up the ones that were still alive and replaced the dead ones. Griff spent a lot of time cutting grass. He maintained their property along with the church's property. A few years ago, when he thought he would be retiring, he decided to volunteer cutting the grass at the church. By not being fully retired, he struggled some weeks to keep both places cut.

Alex's 10-year-old daughter, Gabrielle, decided to join gymnastics again this season. She attended class every Thursday and had hoped Abby and Griff would come watch her first gymnastics meet. Abby remembered how she had spent many nights at that gym with both her daughters, Alex, and Harper, when they were young. They were both highly active and attended gymnastic throughout high school. In fact, Alex was a cheerleader and Harper was on the dance team, so gymnastics helped them both.

Abby decided to go watch Gabby's 1ˢᵗ gymnastics meet, but Griff was not up for it. He said if he never attends another gymnastic event, he would be happy. He said that about cheerleading competitions, too. She couldn't complain because he was a great dad. He was wonderful with the kids and spent a lot of time with them. He made it a point to attend every competition meet and event they had. In addition to their sports activities, he would take them on weekly "Mystery Trips." The trips could be as simple as going for ice cream or a trip to the Global Wildlife refuge in Roberts, Louisiana. They never knew where they were going, but they always knew it was going to be fun. Now that the girls are grown, he continues the Mystery Trips with the grandchildren, but he refuses to endure what he calls 'cruel and unusual punishment'. That was his description of anything to do with cheerleading or gymnastics. Abby guessed he deserved a pass after all those years.

The gymnastics building looked the same as it did several years ago when Abby was last there. Some of the teachers were different, but she recognized a few of them. She spotted Alex and Finn in the bleachers and went to join them. The classes were a lot larger than she remembered.

Gabrielle did a really good job at gymnastics and brought so much energy to her performances. Like most children, she tired from going to practices, but Abby really hoped that Gabrielle would decide to stick with it, because it was so important for children to get physical activity. Too many kids these days stayed on their I-pads or phones playing games. Abby should admit though, that both of her grandkids have always kept a good balance between outside play and technology.

"Mom, do you want to come with us to Mo's Pizza after the meet?" Alex asked Abby.

"Oh, that sounds good. Let me call your dad and see if he wants to join us. He will do whatever he can to avoid coming here, but I'm sure he'll want to come eat with us."

Finn chuckled, "I don't blame him one bit. If I didn't have to be here for Gabby, I wouldn't be. It must be a man thing."

Alex rolled her eyes, "Yeah, lets blame it on that. Anyway, call dad and then let me know. If you want to leave and pick him up, we won't be much longer."

"Alright, I know he'll want to come because I didn't cook dinner tonight. I'll see you there."

Just as she suspected, Griff wanted to join them, so she left to pick him up. Mo's Pizza was a local pizza place with a big selection of pizza and pastas, and they served delicious lasagna. It was a fun place to go after games or practices with the kids. Abby wanted to stay focused on her diet and decided it might be best to order the ½ order of lasagna. Their portions were so big you'd have to bring home your leftovers anyway. She committed to leaving the bread alone. Griff on the other hand, had such strong will power. Abby could never understand how he could go into a place and not order his favorite thing. For her it was a constant battle and always would be.

By the time she picked up Griff and arrived at Mo's, Alex, Finn, and the kids were already there. She didn't realize E.R. would be with them, but he's just like Griff, never passed up a meal. She was excited to see him when they arrived. Abby and Griff didn't get to see him as much as they would have liked.

They placed their order and went over to join them. E.R was the first one up to greet Abby and Griff, as usual. He called them Honey and Papa. He was always so happy to see them, it made Abby's heart glow. He gave Griff a great big hug and kiss. Then he said, "Hey Honey" and hugged and kissed Abby. It's funny how the love you feel for grandkids was simply different than your own kids. It's not that grandparents love the grandkids more, it's just in a "different" way.

"Honey and Papa, I have some good news. I was accepted into the engineering program at the University of New Orleans." E.R. was beaming with pride as he made his announcement.

Abby almost came out of her chair. "That is wonderful news! We are so proud of you. You've been on my mind for a while now. I know how much you wanted this. You are just like your grandfather, very smart and persistent. And I think I'm equally as happy that you will be close to home."

Griff said, "E.R. I'm impressed. I knew you had it in you. Good luck with all the math. That's what I originally thought I wanted to study when I was in college, but I soon learned it was not for me. But math has always been your thing, so I know you'll do great."

Alex chimed in, "They also awarded him a scholarship. Isn't that great news? We're so excited for him."

Abby said, "That's wonderful news. I'm happy for him, I just wish he could've stayed on campus for the first semester. I know he likes living at home, but that would've been a great experience."

Excited, Alex added, "Oh mom, I almost forgot to tell you. We also received a phone call that the apartment has become available. And believe it not it's the one right next door to Piper, the exact one he wanted."

Piper is Abby's great niece. She and E.R are only a month apart in age and have been best friend-cousins forever.

"What? I thought they were completely full," Abby exclaimed.

"They were full. All they said was that something unexpected happened to the person who was supposed to move in it, and it is now available. They were very vague and when I asked questions, they said they were not at liberty to disclose any information."

"Wow, Alex that is a surprise."

Distracted, Abby continued, "I'm so happy for you E.R."

They enjoyed the rest of the evening laughing and talking about the upcoming holidays.

The earlier conversation with Alex and E.R. had rattled Abby's senses. Uneasy, she felt like something was off with the whole apartment thing. Again, is it that she's being paranoid or is there something to be concerned about? Since they arrived home from Mo's, E.R.'s apartment situation was on her mind non-stop.

What could possibly have happened to this kid? Abby wondered. She knew there could be a million reasons why he didn't need the apartment anymore. He could have moved, dropped out, been transferred with a job, family problems, money problems; the list was endless. She just had a sinking feeling in her stomach, and she couldn't shake it. She knew she should just forget about it and be happy for E.R., but for some reason she couldn't.

Abby was usually an optimistic/glass half full kind of girl, but she felt that lately, crazy things were happening that had no rhyme or reason. She didn't want to seem like she was not happy for the turn of events recently, because she was. But she was stuck on the fact that, first, "unexpectedly" Olivia didn't have to move and now E.R. was getting an apartment that was already rented and completely unavailable.

Later, Abby decided to watch some T.V. in order to occupy her mind. Griff always liked to read before he went to bed, but Abby's eyes got so tired at night. And tonight, especially, she didn't want to think about anything.

A short time after Abby sat down to watch television, Griff came into the living room with the newspaper. He liked to read the death notices every night. He always said, "the older we get it seems the more people we know that have passed away."

Sitting with the newspaper open, Griff piped up a little concerned, and said, "Abby, listen to this obituary: *On Monday, September 25, 2017, Samuel Laborde, Jr. passed away at his home from undetermined causes. Sam was born on October 2, 2000, and was 16 years old. He was the devoted son of Samuel Laborde, Sr., and Janet Laborde. He was a senior at Bonnabel High School and planned on attending the University of New Orleans next fall. Relatives and friends are invited to attend the funeral Mass at Lake Lawn funeral home on Friday September 29, 2017, at 11:00am. Interment to follow at Lake Lawn Cemetery. Visitation will begin at 9:00am.*

"Do you think this could be the same kid that was supposed to move into E.R.'s apartment? I don't know why, but this obituary caught my attention. If it's not the same kid, that's a spooky coincidence? Alex said they wouldn't give her any details about it, but doesn't it all seem odd to you?" Griff asked.

Abby was dumbfounded and sat very still. She felt like she couldn't breathe, or even move. Why did this bother her so much? Maybe it was because she had been feeling something was not right lately, and the obituary just validated her suspicions.

Trying not to go into a full-blown anxiety attack, Abby took a few slow breaths and attempted to stay in control. It had been several years since she had an anxiety attack and sometimes, she even wondered if she would ever have to experience another one. For years, she was so out of control with them that it affected her life. Being stuck on Bridges was usually the trigger. She would avoid going across the Mississippi River, if possible. And when she had no way out, she would be sick and worried for days before. She thought she would never be rid of her anxiety until she went to a therapist, Dr. Weber, who taught her some techniques to handle the initial triggers. After months of practicing and learning to be attentive, she felt more in control, and was able to stay in the moment, and avoid more anxiety attacks. *Now, could something as simple as this set me back?* Abby was concerned.

She immediately began to practice what she had learned and was soon able to gain control. Both she and Griff walked into the kitchen, and she sat to talk this out with Griff, who seemed more fascinated than concerned by the whole thing. He was always a very calm person.

A little annoyed at his response to this, Abby said, "A spooky coincidence? Really, that's all you got. Aren't you a little freaked out about this?"

Griff realizing how upset Abby was became concerned about her. She looked a little rattled when he read the obituary, but he didn't realize to what degree. *What's the big deal? It's an unfortunate part of life and things happen every day,* Griff thought.

"What's wrong with you Abby?"

Abby hesitated, and then said, "I don't know exactly. I've had this weird feeling the last few weeks, like something is wrong. I didn't say anything because I knew you would think I was overreacting. Ever since we went to lunch last Tuesday and I saw the man in the Dodge Dart lurking, I can't shake this eerie feeling I have. So, when Olivia called to say they were moving, I thought that was the cause for what I was feeling. Then, when she called to say it all worked out, well that upset me too. And now, with the news from Alex about something happening to some kid and that obituary, I have to say I am concerned. This is all too much; I think it's best if I turn in for the night."

At that, Abby got up and left the room. Her last thought of the night was, *I need to call Olivia so we can get to the bottom of this.*

CHAPTER 7

It was a restless night for Abby, and it seemed like daylight would never come. As soon as the light crept through the window of her bedroom, she jumped up and started getting ready for her morning walk. She wanted to call and invite Olivia to join her but was afraid she was still sleeping. She decided to text her first to see if she was up.

Instead of replying, Olivia called right away. She said that Jack had to go into work early, so they were up at 5:00am and he was out the door by 5:30. Abby told her a little about what was going on and Olivia said she could be there in 20 minutes. Relieved, Abby continued to get ready and waited for her to arrive.

It was one of those mornings that made you realize how lucky you were to be alive and well. The weather was perfect, and the birds sang their angelic songs. The peaceful setting reminded them of the beauty the world had to offer. They just needed to take time to stop and enjoy it. Even with everything going on lately, Abby found such comfort in her surroundings. She and Griff always enjoyed the outdoors.

It was finally Gretna Fest weekend. Abby and Griff looked forward to this all year long. And the weather was spectacular due to a mild cool front that came through the night before. The days warmed up to about 75 degrees and the nights dropped to about 70. In the South, which was considered perfect weather. The headliners were *Kiss*, *Pat Benatar* and *the B 52's*. The plan was to meet Olivia and Jack at their house that evening around 5:00pm and ride together. Later, Alex and her family had planned to meet them at the festival.

"Liv, thanks for coming. I know walking is not one of your favorite things but at least we have nice weather. I'm really excited about Gretna Fest tonight. It seems these days all I want to do is listen to some good music and eat. Thankfully, Gretna Fest offers the best of both. Did I tell you that Alex, Finn, and the kids are coming?"

"Wow, how'd you manage that? Alex isn't too fond of festivals or for that fact, anything that cost a lot of money and requires a lot of walking - except Disney World of course."

Olivia was trying to keep up with Abby, but she was going at a swift pace. It was not that she didn't like exercising because she did. She just would rather be inside her own home or at the gym. Olivia had always been the type of person who could eat whatever she wanted and never gained a pound. She exercised for health reasons, not for maintaining her weight. She knew Abby had struggled with her weight lately and was sure it was from the medication she was on. Abby was just like her until a few years back. When they were young, both were able to eat whatever they wanted, and that habit followed them well into adulthood. They agreed that if they hoped to live into their 90's, they must sustain an active lifestyle. So, with the same goal in mind, exercising was the tool they were using to achieve it.

"Okay, so tell me what's going on now because something has you pretty upset?" Olivia asked with concern in her voice.

Abby sighed, "I haven't been able to piece it all together yet, but yes something is not right. I mentioned to Griff last night that ever since we went to Summit, strange things are happening. And maybe it's just a coincidence, but I don't think so."

"Well Abby, I know you and if you feel something is going on, I trust your instincts. You're usually on target with stuff like that. So, lay it out for me, I'm listening."

"Well, first, when we met a few weeks back at Gattuso's, I noticed a man sitting in a Dodge Dart outside the restaurant. He gave me the creeps. Then, Jack's transfer and how that fell apart because of the bizarre events at the main office. I had hoped and prayed for something to change so you could stay here and next thing I know, it happened. Then E.R. getting into UNO was great and I can accept that he has worked hard and deserved it but, it's well known how difficult that program is to get into. Then, when Alex told me an apartment became available for E.R., the exact one he wanted, that didn't sit well either. But what really threw me for a loop was Griff came across an obituary last night of a young man E.R.'s age. He was supposed to attend UNO, but he was found dead of undetermined causes." Abby tried to stay calm while she was telling this to Olivia.

She continued, "I know it all sounds a little bizarre, but I think somehow the two are related. I really would like to find out more details on both deaths. Maybe if I knew more, I could piece things together and hopefully learn that I'm just overreacting."

Olivia, not wanting to see her best friend upset like this reassured Abby that she was there for her, whatever she needed. "Well, let's go find out what's going on. Where do you want to start? I can get Jack to ask around and maybe get more details on the death of the CEO. Also, maybe we can search the internet for more information on the young man Griff read about last night. At least that's a start."

A feeling of relief came over Abby. She knew she could count on Olivia, to first off, not think she was crazy and secondly, be ready and willing to help. And maybe Jack could find out some information about his CEO.

Since it was Friday and Gretna Fest was that weekend, they decided to enjoy the weekend and dive into things on Monday. It wasn't like they were in a rush or anything. And maybe now, with a plan in place, Abby could relax a little and hopefully get some sleep. While they continued their walk, both of them steered clear of the subject and tried to concentrate on the fun weekend that was ahead.

Almost excitedly, Abby started up, "Did I tell you that Stacy and Greg are going to meet us tonight at Gretna Fest? They were supposed to be out of town, but things changed so they are going to make it. I guess we can meet them at the main stage. Let's bring our chairs and set them on the levee along the river when we get there. Do you have the 'fleur de lis' flag we used last year to mark our spot?"

Olivia responded, "Of course I do. We use that same flag every year. I'll put it in the car when I get home, so I don't forget it. Did you order your tickets online or do you have to buy them at the door? I didn't get around to ordering ours, so we'll have to buy at the door."

"I forgot to order ours, too. With everything going on, I've been a little preoccupied."

With a smirk on her face Olivia announced, "I have some news. Guess whose back in town? I'll give you a hint, he's tall, dark, and handsome and the biggest jerk to ever walk this earth."

"No way! How do you know this? Have you seen him? I bet it's been 30 years or better since he's been back here. Remember how he always used to introduce himself - Randolph Whitmore the IV. It was never, 'Hi, I'm Randy.' I wonder what brought him back here after all these years." Abby said, amused.

Olivia Continued, "I think his Aunt Clara is really ill and the doctors only give her a few days to live. From what I understand, his mother passed on a while back and he hasn't spoken to his sister in years. I didn't realize he kept in touch with his aunt, but I guess there are a lot of things I don't know about him. It's not like we stayed in touch."

Abby, knowing how much Randy hurt Olivia, realized her friend was upset, and rightfully so. He just up and left her one day, without saying goodbye. They were childhood sweethearts and were engaged to be married. He was expected to finish college and join his father's law firm. He did become an attorney, but she didn't know if he ever practiced law. After he left, Olivia had a rough go of it. He was a nice guy and treated her well enough, but Abby never felt like he was the right guy for her. He was a very private person and didn't have a lot of close friends. Sure, they all hung out together, but he never seemed to be enjoying himself.

A few years after he left town, his father died. His mother then moved in with his sister in Florida. Every now and then, someone would bring him up, but she didn't think he had ever contacted any one in their circle of friends. After months of depression and heartbreak, Olivia started to get back to her old self. They would try to do things to keep her busy, but by that time Griff and Abby were married and expecting their first child. That was the plan. They were going to get married and have children at the same time so they could raise them together.

One evening, Abby and Griff had gone to River Shack in Gretna for dinner and to see a band called "Da Rockits" play. Olivia agreed to join them for dinner but didn't want to stay for the band. Right as she got up to leave, Griff ran into one of his old college buddies, Jack. Not wanting to seem rude, Olivia decided to stay for a while longer. She and Jack started talking and the next thing Abby knew, they were dancing and having a good time long into the night. Griff said it was fate that brought them together. Love at first sight. They were inseparable from that night on and were married six months later. They were a match made in heaven and until this day, he had made her incredibly happy.

Olivia and Jack were married just about a year after Randy left. Luckily, she was pregnant with their first child soon after, so Abby and Olivia's plan to have children close in age worked out after all. They never talked about Randy again. He was in Olivia's past and that was where she wanted to leave him.

Now, after all these years, to have him back in town must have felt awkward. There was no doubt she loved Jack, but Abby wondered how Olivia would react if she ran into Randy. Jack knew about Randy, but who knew how he would feel with him around. Abby hoped Randy didn't plan on staying in town for long and that he would leave before anyone ran into him. All Abby could think about was how much he hurt her best friend. She believed what goes around comes around, and while she would never wish harm on anyone, she would love to see him pay for what he put Olivia through.

"Well, just when you think things are crazy enough around here, here comes more trouble. Let's just hope he's here for the funeral and will be gone before we know it. Are you okay?" Abby asked Olivia.

"I'm fine. Jack is the best thing that has ever happened to me, so in a way, I'm thankful for Randy being a jerk. I have so much to be thankful for that there's no room for regret. What was Griff always saying, 'what will be will be'? It would be awkward to see him, but there's nothing Randolph Whitmore the IV can say or do to hurt me anymore. But let's talk about this later, I'm going to head home and get ready for tonight."

"Alright, we'll be at your house for 6:00pm. See you tonight, and Liv, thanks! I love you." Abby and Olivia hugged, and then they parted ways so they could both get ready for the night.

Griff came home from the shop and Abby brought him up to speed about Randy. He would not admit it to Abby, but he always wondered what happened to make Randy leave. Even though they weren't particularly close when they were young, they were together a lot. He never indicated anything was wrong, and Griff never dreamed he would up and leave town like he did. And to leave Olivia without any explanation seemed so cruel. *What could have possibly happened? Did he even love Olivia or was she just convenient?* Secretly, Griff wouldn't mind running into him just to satisfy his curiosity. He hadn't thought about it a lot, but over the years it had popped into his mind a time or two. He hoped for every one's sake, that Abby doesn't run into him. Especially with everything she's been going through, it would not be pretty. No, the best thing for everybody would be for Randy to do whatever he came back here for and to get out of town quickly.

CHAPTER 8

Everyone had been waiting for Gretna Fest all year long. Abby and Griff parked by Olivia's house and rode with them since parking was usually pretty limited. They made their way to the main stage and set up their chairs. Alex, Finn, and Gabrielle were there and E.R. was coming a little later.

After they settled down, everyone wanted to go get some food and something to drink. A lot of the local places had booths set up and the food was always good. Griff and Abby decided to visit the Italian Village. They made a great shrimp pasta dish but sometimes they'd run out, so Griff and Abby tried to get there early.

That was exactly what Abby needed. It always reminded her of her teenage years when they would go to City Park for outdoor concerts. Sometimes they would go out to the New Orleans lake front and enjoy the music there. Music always had a special place, not only in her heart, but in her soul. It made her feel alive. There was a song for any occasion.

Griff, with a smirk on his face looked at Abby, "Let's dance!" Knowing full well it was too crowded for dancing, he grabbed her hand and pulled her close.

Abby backed up, "Come on, you know it's too crowded for that." She'd been noticing the crowd thickening by the minute. *It must be the beautiful weather bringing everybody out tonight.*

"Look, there's Stacy and Greg. I think they saw us." Griff waved.

Abby turned to look but couldn't see over the crowd. A few seconds later she spotted Stacy. "I'm so glad you could make it. It wouldn't be the same without you guys."

"I know, ever since I found out we were supposed to be out of town this weekend, I've been so upset," Stacy laughed. "I couldn't believe it when his business trip was postponed. I think he was happy about it too. He doesn't like to admit it, but he likes it when we can all get together the way we used to. Did you eat already?"

"So far we sampled the shrimp fettuccini. Griff went to get in line for a cannoli and I know he wants to get over to the charbroiled oyster booth next. I think I might get a turkey leg myself. Let's walk and see what else they have. Olivia and Jack are around here somewhere. Oh, and Alex and her family are here. She'll be excited to see you. Harper will probably come later with her friends. We seldom see her these days. She's always running with her friends and doesn't seem to have much time for us."

"How is everyone doing? I know E.R is graduating this year, but how old is Gabby now? I haven't seen them in years. And is Harper finished with school?"

"Gabby is nine now and in fourth grade. She's as active as ever and smart as a whip. Alex is probably over by the rides with her now. E.R. is on his way. He had a few things to do, so he stayed back and will drive himself here. Wait till you see how tall and handsome he is. I still can't believe he's growing up so quickly. Stacy, we're getting old." Just then, Abby's phone rang. It was E.R. looking for his mother. He said he tried to call her, but she didn't answer. He had a flat tire on Fourth Street just before the bridge in Harvey. He wanted to let her know. A man stopped to help him, and they were finished fixing it. He was on his way now.

"I'll let your mother know as soon as I see her. Be careful and call us when you get in the festival. We'll be by the food booths. I'm going get a turkey leg, so I'll get you one. See you soon, love you. Bye."

Abby always worried about him out on the road. He and Harper were only 2 years apart and with both driving now, Abby was a nervous wreck. She had to admit, E.R was a pretty careful driver. Now Harper on the other hand drove way too fast. Once, Harper was bringing Abby to meet Griff at Harrah's Casino in New Orleans on a Friday afternoon. They left Marrero at five pm, the busiest time of the day to go across the river, and arrived at Harrah's by five thirteen. Usually, on a good day without traffic, it would take at least 25 minutes. Abby swore she would never ride with her again and from that day since, she hadn't. When they go for lunch or shopping, they each take their own vehicles.

Noticing Abby in deep thought, Stacy pointed out the turkey leg booth. While they were in line, they talked about different people they had run into, and others they were sure to see throughout the night.

"Did you know Randy was back in town?" Stacy asked as she read the booth menu. "We ran into him at the gate. At first, we weren't sure it was him but as we got closer, we realized it was."

Abby stopped dead in her tracks. "He's here? He's at the festival? Why would he come here after the way he left town? We need to find Olivia and warn her. She knew he was back, but we thought it was just because his Aunt Clara was sick. Clearly, he wasn't in a hurry to leave again. I told E.R. to meet us here, so let me go get Griff to wait for him and then we'll go find Liv."

Abby guessed they were too late by the look on Olivia's face. But Randy was nowhere around so Abby wasn't sure if they ran into each other, or she just knew that he was at the festival? Either way, Olivia looked like she saw a ghost and was noticeably upset.

"Hey Liv, are you okay?" Abby put an arm around her and spoke softly.

"He's here. Why would he come here?" Olivia said staring into space, visibly in shock. "He knows we come every year, so he had to figure he would run in to me at some point. Did he want that to happen? I can't see him right now because I don't know what I'd say or do. I still have so much anger inside of me and I don't know why. I love how my life turned out. I love my husband. I can honestly say I have no feelings for Randy except contempt. And I think I actually feel pity for him, living alone away from his family all this time."

Abby was a little confused. "Liv, did you run into him?"

Olivia, a bit more coherent now said, "No, thank God. I was walking to the food booths to meet you and I saw him coming in the gate. Luckily, he didn't see me, so I turned and came back here."

"When we got here, we saw him at the gate," announced Stacy. "I can't believe he's back after all this time."

"What do you want to do? We can leave if you want to. Stacy, maybe Griff and Jack can get a ride back with you and Greg later," Abby said in a supportive tone.

"Absolutely, whatever you want to do Olivia. We're here for you sweetie." Stacy reassured her.

"I am not leaving and will not let Randy or anybody else ruin this weekend for us. I'll be alright. Again, I just wouldn't know what to say to him. I guess after all this time, there's not a lot to say. I just don't want Jack to feel awkward about it. Of course, he knows the whole story and he definitely knows how much I love him. We even joked about how grateful we both were that Randy took off like he did. I didn't think I would ever see him again, so it took me by surprise. I just want to go find the guys and enjoy this night with my best friends. And just so you both know; it means the world to me to have you by my side."

"Well then, you know the guys are probably still at the charbroiled oyster booth. Let's go find them." Having said that, Abby grabbed Olivia and Stacy's hands and together they walked to the food area.

It turned out to be such a beautiful night. The main stage was on the other side of the levee, right on the banks of the Mississippi river. The warmth that was in the air was replaced by an autumn breeze. The air coming off the river was crisp and refreshing. It was like a friendly touch that made you feel welcomed, and everything felt brand new.

They found their seats and spent the evening laughing, joking, and enjoying each other's company. The headlining band at the main stage was *Huey Lewis & the News*. They put on an amazing show.

Alex and Finn found them, and they all enjoyed Gabby and her endless energy running up and down the levee. She loved to dance, so she and Griff danced to most of the songs. E.R. finally made it and after hanging with his friends for a while, he came and joined them. The band finished playing and it had gotten late, but the group stuck around waiting for the crowd to die down. The guys were sitting around talking about fishing, school, work, and other guy stuff, while the girls were talking about the upcoming holidays.

Jack said, "I can't believe how quick the time passed tonight. E.R., your mom said you had a flat tire. Was this the first time you had a flat?"

E.R. looked annoyed, and said, "Yes it was. Papa showed me how to change a flat and check my oil a long time ago, but I never had to do it on my own. Thankfully, this man stopped and helped me. I could've done it by myself, but I was glad for the help. Oh, and Papa, you remember that car we saw at the Vicari Auction last year that I liked? I think it was a Dodge Dart. Well the man who helped me was driving one like that. I think he said it was a 1964. That's a cool little car."

Griff's eyes met Abby's and he knew what she was thinking. Before, he thought she was just being paranoid, but now he's getting a little concerned himself because there really weren't a lot of Dodge Darts in the area.

As Griff turned it over in his mind, he said, "Yes, I remember the car. They always have unique cars at the auction every year. What else did the man say to you? Was he someone you knew or just a random stranger that stopped to help?"

"When I realized the tire was flat, I pulled over to check it. Just a few minutes later he pulled up behind me. I've never seen him before in my life, but he seemed nice enough. He said he was from Mississippi and was in town for a few weeks. Do y'all know someone who drives that type of car?"

"No, I was simply curious to know if you recognized him. You know you have to be so careful these days," answered Griff.

"Papa, you know I had it under control, thanks to you. Because of the festival, it was bumper to bumper traffic.

There were people walking everywhere trying to get here. If the man was up to no good, he picked a bad place to do it. Besides, you also taught me to take care of myself." E.R. flexed his muscles at Griff and said, "These 'guns' aren't for nothing."

Everyone couldn't help but laugh. Leave it to E.R. to lighten up the mood. He took after Abby for that. He was always upbeat, but sometimes too upbeat. *Just like most kids today, he wouldn't know danger when he saw it,* thought Griff. *But then again, we were probably all like that when we were young.*

The crowds were almost gone, and they decided it was time to call it a night. Fortunately, they never did run into Randy, but there were two more days left of the festival. Perhaps, he wouldn't return and would instead just leave town, but not likely.

CHAPTER 9

The rest of the weekend went by without any big surprises. The Gretna Fest was a big success, as usual. *Kiss* was the headliner Saturday night, and everyone enjoyed them. After a weekend like that, it took a while to recuperate. The last thing any of them wanted to do was exercise, including Abby. She did "sleep in" a little, but once she woke on Monday morning, she was ready to get moving, and headed out for her walk.

Olivia didn't commit to the walk that morning, but she did agree to meet Abby for lunch. They were going to hatch out a plan to investigate all the strange things going on lately. This was nothing new for either of them. Anytime something didn't sit well with them, they set out to fix it. This problem was no different; in fact, with Google, they should be able to research events even from Houston, since that was where Jack's CEO was from, and hopefully not have to go there.

On that morning Abby had a tough time walking. Gretna Fest was always fun, but she was whipped out from all the walking at the festival. She had been watching what she eats lately, but the past weekend messed that up. She couldn't stop thinking about all the things that happened. She couldn't believe Randy was back in town. Olivia seemed to put it aside and have a good time at Gretna Fest, but it bothered her more than she let on. Hopefully, he's going to finish up what he came here for and leave town before things get ugly. *I will not stand for Olivia getting hurt again, so one way or another, he has to go.* And what were the chances of E.R. getting help from someone that drove the same kind of car as the man she thought was following her. No, that was no coincidence and today they were going to look into that, too.

Abby finished up her walk and headed home to get ready to go meet Olivia for lunch.

#

Abby and Olivia met at River Shack in Gretna. They usually went to Gattuso's, but Olivia felt like having 'Garbage Fries', an appetizer at River Shack. They take French fries and pile on cheese, onions, jalapenos, mushrooms, and roast beef debris. It was sinful, but it was that kind of a day

"Okay, so where do we start?" Olivia asked.

"Well, let's start at the beginning with Jacks transfer. Did you get him to ask around about his CEO's death?"

"I did ask him, but he didn't have any information as of this morning. By the time I called him Friday, he was already about to leave for the weekend. Hopefully, today he'll get time to talk to more people. What about the internet? Let's look online because they might have an article about it that we missed." Olivia opened her I-pad and searched: Freddie Jones, Houston, Texas.

The waitress came over and they placed their order for drinks and an appetizer. River Shack was crowded for a weekday. It was a fairly new restaurant in the area, which usually meant they would be crowded for a while. They had a nice upstairs area that was open and overlooked the Mississippi River. It was nice to sit out there in the fall. Also, they usually had bands on the weekends, just like Gattuso's, which was just down the street.

"Look at this article in The Houston Chronicles. It says:

CEO of a major company found dead in his home, yesterday. Mr. Fredrick Jones, the CEO of Offshore Solutions, was found dead in his home yesterday. Jones's wife found him on the floor of his home office around 2pm. When she realized he was unresponsive, she immediately called 911. At first, cause of death was thought to be suicide but later ruled undetermined causes. His wife said, "Freddie was dedicated to running and worked out every morning before work. He was preparing for a trip to Spain next year with friends for "The Running of the Bulls." He was especially excited about the merging of the two branches of his company happening later this year." She said, "It was unusual for him to be home in the middle of the day." Fredrick Jones was 36 years old.

"Well that doesn't help much." Abby picked at the garbage fries. "One thing's for sure; he had a lot to live for. According to his wife, he was happy, full of life and making plans for the future. What a tragedy."

"Yeah, from what his wife said, I would rule out suicide too. I don't think you would be making future plans if you weren't planning on being around. Maybe there's no mystery here, Abby. I know it seems like a lot of strange things happening lately, but maybe they are just coincidences."

Abby nodded, with concern all over her face. "I know it's farfetched, but Liv, something is not right, I can feel it. Let's see if there is anything, we can find on that young man that was supposed to go to UNO. I think his name was Samuel Laborde, Jr. and he was from Metairie."

The waitress came over again and asked for their orders. They decided to split a cheeseburger since the garbage fries were so filling. Besides, Abby's appetite was not what it usually was with all the stress lately and her nerves were getting the best of her. They continued to search for answers and discussed where to go after lunch.

Driving towards Lake Lawn Cemetery, Abby had a strange feeling come over her. She had been feeling like someone was watching her. It could have been because of that Dodge Dart she'd spotted a few times. It did seem as if the man was looking at her, and then to have the person that helped E.R drive the same type of car, was disturbing to say the least.

She had been so on edge lately that the slightest thing made her jump. Just that morning, Griff came around the corner in the kitchen and she almost threw her plate at him. She was glad it was Monday and she and Olivia could start to figure out what was going on.

Olivia had been very patient with all of this. She didn't have the same feeling Abby did about everything but trusted that Abby had a good sense about her and wouldn't be so adamant if it were nothing. There was probably a good explanation for all of it, they just needed to figure it out and she was confident they would. Olivia was not sure what Abby thought they'd find at the cemetery, but it couldn't hurt to go. It was not her favorite place to go, so she was a little apprehensive. Truth be told she was downright afraid, because unlike Abby, she does not like scary movies or anything creepy. Good ol' romance movies made her happy and didn't keep her up at night. Olivia was hoping they could get in and out quickly.

The cemetery was right off the interstate, so they arrived quickly and parked. The cemetery was not busy at all, probably because it was Monday. Often, the graves were above the ground because New Orleans is below sea level, but Lake Lawn provided both in ground and above ground options. While it was a beautiful and peaceful place, it was also a little eerie. There was something about being among the dead that sparked a little anxiety in everyone. Even the bravest got a little spooked when walking among the graves.

There were rows and rows of tombstones that stood tall, erect, as if at attention. All full of bodies that once roamed this earth, with unfinished stories, now empty of life. The smell of freshly mowed grass and of flowers decorating the lovingly kept graves, lingered in the air. It was tranquil and dignified, but at the same time felt lonely, cold, and barren. It reminded Abby of the delicacy of life.

Earlier, at River shack, Olivia searched Google for Samuel Laborde's obituary. In the article, it said today was his birthday. They figured someone would show up at the gravesite and then they could, respectfully of course, talk to them about what happened. Every little bit of information brought them one step closer to an explanation they so desperately sought.

As they walked along the rows of tombstones, they listened carefully for a sign of someone around. It was unusually quiet to the point of deafening. The breeze kicked up every now and then with the sound of a low whistle. The sun was out, full, and bright, casting long dark shadows along their path as they searched for new burial sites. This was not where Olivia thought she would be today.

"Listen. It sounds like voices on the next row." Olivia pointed, "Let's turn there and maybe we can see where they are. With the wind around here, they could sound closer than they actually are."

At that very moment, Abby stopped dead in her tracks. All color drained from her face as she opened her mouth only to realize she was speechless. Quickly, she grabbed Olivia's hand and pulled her down beside her.

"There's someone following us." She whispered, "Look over there, the shadow of a man. I noticed it when we first started walking, but assumed it was just someone here to visit a loved one. But every turn we make, he makes and when we stop, he stops. What should we do?"

Olivia, horrified because of the situation they were in, gathered herself, then looked around to see which way they should go. If they continued on the path they were on, they would have ended up at the back of the cemetery, which seemed darker and more isolated. She noticed the shadow but was not completely convinced it was following them. It could have been anybody, but the question was, do they approach him and find out? That could end up being a bad decision if she were wrong.

Olivia decided they should slowly walk toward the voices they heard earlier, but then realized she didn't hear them anymore. "Have they left already or maybe they're just having a moment of silence?" Either way, that choice no longer seemed to make sense. She took out her cell phone and held it up.

"What are you doing?" Abby grabbed Olivia's arm.

"I'm going to take a picture of whoever it is and send it to Jack."

"What is he going to do with that? We need help here, now Olivia. We need a plan now."

"If I'm going to be murdered today, at least they will know who did it. Olivia proudly added, "I saw that in one of those stupid horror movies you make me go see."

Not amused, Abby turned to her and motioned for her to run on the count of three. Chances were whoever it was wouldn't have time to catch up, since they were not that far from the entrance. Once they were safe and around other people, they could try to figure out who it was and what they wanted. Without a doubt, Abby knew he was following them.

Abby counted down and they ran as fast as they could to the end of the row they were in. As they turned the corner, still running, they smacked right into someone, and both let out a scream that was heard all over the cemetery. Quickly realizing that it was the security guard, Abby looked back to see the shadow of the man just disappearing around the back corner. For a split second, she considered running after him, but thought better of it. If he got away, they may never find out who it was.

As they gathered themselves and apologized to the security guard, they filled him in on what had happened. He tried to assure them that he just finished his rounds and the only people he saw left in the cemetery were Olivia and Abby. After a while of convincing him, someone was there, he escorted them to the front office and agreed to go out and investigate the grounds.

About 20 minutes passed, then the security guard returned to report that the cemetery was completely empty. He offered to call the police to make a report if they wanted, but both Abby and Olivia declined the offer.

Back in the car now and on their way back to the Westbank of the river, where they both lived, neither one said a word. It took them a while to calm down and reflect on what actually happened. Things turned out fine, but what if that security guard wasn't around? What if the man they ran into was the man following them? The thought of, "what if" had them rattled to the core. It was time to go home and tell their husbands where they went and what happened. They expected that conversation to be fun.

Right before they got back to Olivia's car her phone rang. She answered and found Stacy on the other end of the line. Olivia listened to what she had to say and then they hung up. She sat there for a moment, with a stunned look on her face, unable to talk. Abby realized something must have been wrong and she waited for Olivia to share the news with her. Afterwards, they both sat in the car, in silence and wondered when this would all end and how much more they could justify as coincidence.

CHAPTER 10

SEPTEMBER 1977

Detective Clay Hawkins stepped out of his car and into what seemed like a hornets' nest. He didn't have time to enjoy his morning coffee before his pager was buzzing on his side. He called the office and was informed that a body was found in the woods over by I-55. He was already up and dressed ready for work, so he was out the door quickly and was one of the first to arrive at the crime scene.

The sun was slowly rising over the trees and the dew dripped from the branches, soaking the ground. The woods still possessed the quiet of dawn only to be disturbed by the arrival of the investigation team. It was a scene right out of a book, less the bloody remains of a body motionless on the ground. Shortly after, the yellow tape went up, and the place was crawling with every law enforcement agency in the area.

Just behind the row of pine trees, about 20 yards away, was a walking trail, which could explain why the victim was out here in the middle of nowhere that early in the morning. On that particular morning, the trail was empty and showed no apparent sign of anything suspicious. That was where Detective Hawkins came in because he was the best.

Since the first murder investigation that he led back in 1967, he had become obsessed with leaving no stone unturned. That first case was as difficult as they come and almost drove him crazy. It was a big part of the reason he was never married. There was a time he was involved with someone, in fact, almost engaged. The night that he was going to pop the question at their favorite restaurant was the same night of those gruesome murders a decade ago. Needless to say, he never made it to the restaurant, and since that night, he was obsessed with the case. They simply drifted apart. He didn't blame her, and she still held a special place in his heart.

After the end of Detective Hawkins dwindling relationship, he had entertained plenty of women but never again found the love he once felt. He was resolved to the fact that as long as he stayed with the Department, he probably never would. He often thought about leaving, but after every case he solved, he felt more and more fulfilled. When he made the decision to become a detective, he did it because he wanted to help people find justice. Like his grandfather before him, who died in the line of duty, he felt it was his duty to serve and protect.

He was raised by his grandparents, after his mother and stepfather were killed by a drunk driver when he was five years old. They gave him so much love and support that he never really felt like he missed out on anything in life. Sure, he dreamed about what his parents were like, but he had no memory of them. As far as he was concerned, his grandparents were his parents, and he couldn't have loved them anymore. His grandmother always said he had a sixth sense about things, and she knew he would make a wonderful detective one day. Both had passed, and Detective Hawkins knew that without them, his life probably would've gone in a completely different direction. He had seen what it was like for children to not have the family love, and support they deserve. He saw this tragic situation frequently in his line of work when the victims in his cases had children and no living relatives. He knew exactly how lucky he was, and he knew he owed everything to his grandparents.

Detective Hawkins still remembered that first case back in 1967. Two people were found beaten to death and the third was thought to be the suspect. The problem was that the suspect was an elderly man who had no memory of the murders and was in critical condition himself. After months of investigating, he was charged with the murders, but his lawyers claimed temporary insanity. He remembered feeling sorry for the old man. During his investigation, he concluded that something changed in the old man after he had his stroke, because everything Detective Hawkins dug up pointed to an upstanding citizen and genuinely nice guy. He remembered, shortly before the murders the suspect had a stroke, but he was in rehab and worked really hard to get out of his wheelchair and walk again. The old man did finally manage to walk again and was only using a cane to walk at the time of the murders. The man never recovered from the stress and guilt of the murders he was accused of, and he died before he made it to his trial.

One thing that still bothered Detective Hawkins so many years later, was that in the hospital, the man kept mumbling "look within" and "be careful," over and over again. Later, the man had no recollection of saying anything at all, much less knowing what those phrases meant. So that lead, if you want to call it that, went cold.

Looking at the body of the victim in the woods that morning reminded Detective Hawkins of the crime scene in 1967. The amount of blood and the mangled mess the body was left in was similar. The only difference was that it was only one body. It was apparent that the murder weapon was some blunt object, which out there in the woods could be a large branch or maybe a rock. They wouldn't know until the coroner completed their autopsy and declared the cause of death. Until the word came from the coroner, every inch of woods was searched, and all available manpower worked to find answers.

CHAPTER 11

Once again, Abby woke, having had a rough night's sleep the night before. That seemed to be the norm for her. This lack of sleep made it difficult to get up and do her morning walk. Some days, she just wanted to skip it and stay in bed. Looking out the kitchen window, she noticed that everything was wet, and raindrops were dripping from the tree branches. It must have rained overnight. She quickly grabbed a bottle of water and her walking stick and headed for the door. Sometimes after a rain, the sun would come out making it hotter than usual, so she wanted to be finished before that happened.

Today, she had planned to have lunch with Harper. They tried to spend time together every Tuesday. They were both so busy, especially Harper, who was just starting out with her career. Abby was just grateful her youngest daughter set time aside for her. Griff complained that he never saw her anymore, so he did join them sometimes. Harper was at that age where everything else in the world was more important than mom and dad, so they took what they could get. Harper loved to go to hibachi, so they agreed to meet at a restaurant called Fuji Hana's around 11:30.

The morning was heating up with the sun peeking through the trees. Still it was such a beautiful morning, and you could hear the birds chirping. She was halfway through her walk when she heard what sounded like a car coming up the street, so Abby tried to stay on the side, out of the way. There were no sidewalks in Crown Point, so the only place to walk was on the street.

Abby remembered that Harper was going to Baton Rouge to take her state board exam later that week. From what they were told, most people do not pass the first time, so they were hoping for the best. Passing it the first time around would be so rewarding for her. She didn't show it, but Harper was a little nervous. Anyone who knew her knew that she was the most laid-back person in the world. She was always a free spirit and Abby loved that about her, except, when it came across as not caring. There was a fine line there and she would have to figure it out. *Either way,* Abby thought, *she would complete the exam, and we'll see how it goes.*

Harper was hoping to further her training with classes in New York. She definitely found her calling and was already one of the best makeup artists in the area. When she first approached her parents about going to school for makeup and not going to college, they were a little apprehensive. That industry had grown so much over the years. It was amazing how many people paid top dollar to get their makeup done. So, they figured she could try this and could always go back to college if she wanted too. They were so glad it worked out for her, and were very proud parents. They were confident that she would pass her state boards, and then she would be on her way to New York.

Abby had been trying not to think about all the crazy stuff that had been going on, but the experiences and memories kept creeping back into her thoughts. She usually enjoyed her walks, which were an opportunity for her to reflect on the things going on in her life, but she was trying not to think too much. Again, she heard the sound of a car, but never did see it pass. Sometimes, you could hear cars on the highway, and they sound like they were next to you. It was probably on the next street.

Thankfully, her walk came to an end, and she wanted to get ready so she could go meet Harper and enjoy lunch with her daughter. Abby, knowing Harper would probably be late, stopped to get gas on her way to the restaurant. Fuji Hanna Restaurant doesn't like to seat you until your entire party was there. She walked in and was shocked to see Harper there waiting on her. They sat down and started making small talk while they were deciding what to order. Harper looked a little preoccupied, so Abby asked out of concern if everything was alright.

"Yeah, I'm okay. I'm just worried about passing my exam."

"Harper, you are ready for your big test. I know you can do this. Just relax, take a deep breath, and take your time." Again, Abby noticed her daughter was distracted, but this time was distracted by a boy who just walked in."

"Do we know him?" Abby joked.

"Mom!" Harper rolled her eyes at her mother adding, "What are you talking about?"

"I'm talking about the young man that just walked in who you can't stop looking at. He's really good looking. Where do you know him from?"

"I met him the other day for the first time. His name is Noah Doucet, and he has an accent like he's from Cut Off or down the bayou somewhere. I don't know that much about him, but I think his dad is a lawyer. Mom, stop looking over there!"

Abby picked up her phone and said, "Let's pull him up on Facebook."

"No, mom, stop! That's creepy stalker stuff. You're so weird sometimes. Promise me you won't look him up. Anyway, I think he's new in town. Can we just order please, you're embarrassing me?" With that, Harper picked up the menu and ignored her mom.

Abby was thrilled at the prospect of someone new in Harper's life. Her last steady boyfriend, Ted, was when she was in high school. They parted ways when he left for college and announced that he didn't want to be tied down anymore. Harper was upset at first, but she was probably relieved because he was still so immature. She knew they had different goals in life and while Harper came to this realization early on, she wasn't ready to end it. He definitely did her a favor. Despite her excitement, Abby decided to move on but not without storing his name in her memory. She would respect her daughter's wishes and honor the promise she made and not look him up on her

Facebook. When she got home, she would just call Olivia and get her to do it.

They both ordered and talked about school, her sister Alex and everything except Noah. Harper did well in keeping her cool and acting like she didn't see him. A little later, he walked up to the table, and she almost choked on her food. Before he even noticed her shock, she quickly recovered and was able to talk. He introduced himself to Abby and reminded Harper of their first encounter. Evidently, he must have tried to talk to her, but she was busy dancing with her girlfriends and ignored him. He asked how they were, and then as a little dig, told Harper "Wow look at you, still living and breathing and not one of your girlfriends around." Abby was about to ask him to join them when and older man walked in and called him. Harper looked ready to tear into him, so it was probably for the best.

He said, "Well, I just wanted to say hi and I hope to see you around sometime." With that said, he turned and left.

Harper gave Abby that look that said, "Mom, don't say a word!" So of course, she did. Abby tried to encourage Harper to go give him her phone number but the horrified look on her face told her she wouldn't. Hopefully, they would run into each other again and be able to have a little time for conversation. It would be good for Harper.

Abby really enjoyed her lunch with Harper. It was just what she needed, light conversation and laughter. After lunch, they went to do a little Christmas shopping. Every year, Abby tried to get all her shopping done early for everyone on her list except Griff, Harper, and Alex. She usually liked to put special thought into their gifts and with all the others out of the way, it took the pressure off.

Christmas had always been a big deal in the Stewart household. With the kids grown and Alex having a family of her own, it hadn't felt the same for a couple of years now, but that didn't stop Abby from keeping their traditions alive. Actually, the Stewart family went all out to celebrate all holidays and next up was Halloween.

They went back to Huey P. Long Street in Gretna, to a charming little boutique called "Fleurty Girl." They sold a lot of cute things that celebrate New Orleans and other local stuff. You could find unique things there and that was exactly what Abby was looking for. It seemed that lately, everyone loved things that said NOLA, or anything that had streetcars or snowballs on it. "504", which represented their area code, was really popular; anything with New Orleans or Louisiana on it, as well. They sold hats, shirts, jewelry, home décor and so many other things. Even if you're not looking to buy something, just walking through the store felt good and usually brought back childhood memories. Who doesn't remember going for snowballs with the whole family in the summer? Finally home after her lunch outing, Abby decided to relax on the sofa for a while and think about the Halloween Party they host every year. Halloween would fall on Tuesday that year, so the party would be on Saturday, October 28, which was less than a month away.

This year Harper actually seemed excited about it and even offered to help. The past few years it was difficult to get her to attend at all, much less help plan it.

The guest list was typically easy because Abby and Griff could use the one from the previous year and adjust. This year, they were going to have a Masquerade Costume Party. It was so much fun when people dressed up and you had to figure out who they were and equally fun when that proved to be difficult. Griff was really good at fooling everyone because he chose crazy costumes. He had no problem throwing on a wig and a dress and becoming Elsa from Frozen or Beyoncé. Of course, he always put the Halloween twist on any costume.

Abby loved everything about having a party, including planning it, executing the plans, and enjoying the day. When the kids were young, they would have a haunted house for the guest. That was always fun and most of the kids enjoyed it. It had been years since Abby and Griff had a haunted house, but Griff would die if she suggested it this year. It was a lot of work but totally worth it. She decided she'd have to think about that idea for a while.

For now, Abby started with the menu. Since it was cool outside, they'd definitely have a soup and hot chocolate. She learned a long time ago to keep it simple with the food because even though she asks her guest not to, everyone ends up bringing a dish. It was all part of the Halloween spirit, and it was fun to see how creative people were with the food. There were so many ideas online that you could find on sites like Pinterest if you wanted to theme food.

After a while, Abby fell asleep and didn't wake up until she heard her phone ring. It was Olivia, and she sounded frantic.

CHAPTER 12

Abby stood shocked as she listened carefully. "Randy didn't make it," Olivia said to Abby on the other end of the line. "Oh my God Abby, Stacy just called to tell me that he passed earlier today. It's so sad you know. He was all his poor aunt had left. When Stacy called the other day and told us about his accident, I never imagined he would die. The fact that he was missing for a few days and found alive was bizarre, but to survive all that and still die is so heart wrenching. When I saw him at the Gretna Fest Friday, I didn't realize that would be the last time I would see him."

"Are you okay? Abby said, while searching for the right words to continue. "I know it was a long time ago and he really hurt you, but you did love the guy once."

"It just came as a shock. I think I just feel sorry for him. He never really moved on and it seems his life was kind of sad. Well, what is that saying, 'what goes around comes around'?"

The hair on Abby's arms stood up and her heart felt like it would pop out of her chest. The words her best friend just said to her made her uneasy. *Wasn't that my exact thought a few days before?* When Abby found out

Randy was back in town, she was still so upset with him. At the time she didn't say anything to Olivia, but she was thinking how she wished he would pay for what he did. Now he's dead. Again, it's probably just all the Halloween stuff Abby was thinking about earlier that made her overreact.

"Liv, I had that exact thought when we were walking the other day. Do you think that maybe that's not a coincidence?"

If Olivia shared the same concern about it, she gave no indication. "That seems a bit of a stretch don't you think. But just in case, don't have any ill thoughts about me, okay. No, I think it was just Randy's time to go. I think I'm just in shock about it all, but I'm fine. I'll let you know if I hear anything else. Anyway, I had a message from you earlier about looking up someone on Facebook. What was that about?"

Abby did have to laugh at herself for thinking her thoughts were somehow responsible for Randy getting his payback. Olivia always knew how to take the edge off.

"Earlier at lunch with Harper, a young man came in and she immediately took notice. I could see she was really interested in him, but you know Harper, she told me I was crazy and tried to distract me. He did end up seeing her and he came to the table. He is a really good-looking young man. She said she met him earlier and thought he was from out of town. Liv, he definitely was interested in her, you could see it in his eyes, the way he looked at her.

But of course, when I suggested looking him up, she freaked out! She made me promise not to."

"So, now I'm looking him up, right?"

"You know me so well." Abby smiled and said, "His name is Noah Doucet, and he has a strong Cajun dialect like he's from Cut Off, Louisiana or somewhere down the bayou toward Grand Isle. He's tall and has dark brown hair and the most gorgeous blue eyes."

"Well then, I bet this is him. I'll send you a picture right now. It says here he just graduated from Loyola University and is currently single. Did you get the text I just sent?"

Abby looked at the message from Olivia and was excited to confirm that it was him.

"That's him! Don't you think he's cute and perfect for Harper? We must find a way to make sure they meet up again. Harper was a little infuriated when he called her out about her friends, but I like that about him. We both know friends are the best, but you have to make time for love. I could tell he got under her skin, but she liked it. No one has been able to capture her attention like that for an awfully long time. This could be interesting."

"Here we go again. You know she's going to be mad as hell if she finds out you are interfering. But that's never stopped you before. I'll see what else I can find out about him and call you later."

"Thanks Liv. Talk to you soon." Abby was so excited at the prospect of a new boyfriend for Harper that she forgot the feeling she had earlier about Randy. This would be a nice distraction from all the strange things that have been bothering her. And yes, Harper would have a fit if she knew Abby was meddling but that's the thing, she's never going to find out.

With that thought in mind, Abby's phone rang, and it was Harper. She felt a sense of guilt come over her and considered not answering it. She knew it would be impossible for Harper to know about her meddling already and it could be something serious, so she answered it.

"Mom, are you there?"

"Hey Harper, what's up?" Abby held her breath for the first second every time Harper called afraid something was wrong.

"Nothing much, I was just thinking about the Halloween party. How many people can I invite? Henley just called and said we were invited to a party at Republic this weekend and I wanted to tell some of my other friends so they can get a costume. The party is the same weekend as Voodoo Fest but the lineup for Saturday isn't that good, so we can go early and come afterwards."

Henley Kerner had been Harper's best friend since kindergarten. Those two had gotten into more messes throughout their 20 years and still were inseparable. They went to the same schools and danced at the same place. Every vacation they took as a family, Henley was with them. She was *that* person for Harper, her "go to" person. She was like a sister to her and a part of the family. Harper and her sister Alex were 17 years apart, so it was nice for her to have Henley. In fact, Alex's son E.R. was only 2 years younger than Harper and was always more like a brother to her than a nephew. They always fought like brother and sister growing up and have remained close. It sounded like our party was about to make a shift to cater to younger people with Harper and E.R. now taking an interest.

Abby smiled at the thought of her whole family enjoying the party this year. "Harper, you can invite whoever you want but keep in mind it's at the house, so we are limited. How many people do you have in mind?"

"I think it will probably be about twenty at the most and I know it's at the house mom." Harper sounding annoyed added, "It's not like I'm going to invite everyone. I know there's a limit. I'll talk to a few people this weekend and get a better idea. So, it's okay to invite around twenty, right?"

"Absolutely, I am so excited that you will be a part of it this year. I have always wanted you kids to join us, but I understood that a party with the parents was not appealing to you as a teenager. And by the way, I think the theme is going to be Morgus the Magnificent. Do you remember watching the reruns when you were little? It was Dad's idea, but I really like it. We'll use that as the theme for the whole party and we're going to decorate the house like a science laboratory. Maybe next week we can go shopping for costumes. I need a lab coat that I can dirty up with blood and stuff and a crazy wig. And remember most of all it's a masquerade party. Please ask your friends to wear mask. It's okay if they don't, but at least try to get them to do it. That is usually the best part of the costume. I have to go; someone's at the door. Let me know the count when you have a better idea. I love you."

Abby went to open the door, but there was no one there, just an envelope with no name on it. Probably the mailman left it when she took so long to answer. But that's odd, why would he not just put it in the mailbox.

Abby had been so rattled by the strange things happening lately that she was almost afraid to open the envelope. Should she wait for Griff to get home first? She put the envelope on the table and stared at it. *What could it be and who could it be from?*

With her overactive imagination she thought of the anthrax scare a few years back. People were sending anthrax through the mail and people were dying from it. She immediately ran and washed her hands.

Okay Abby don't be so ridiculous. Now you're acting like a crazy person. It's been years since all that happened and besides, who would send you anthrax. Where do you even get anthrax? Abby was trying to justify feeling so anxious and was trying to reason with herself. Then, she recalled a while back on the news that people were getting packages left on their porches with bombs in them. But this is an envelope not a package. She paced back and forth and with each pass she became more anxious. *Should I call Griff? He'll just think I'm nuts. And if I call Olivia, she'll come right over but what if it's something bad. Oh, the hell with it.* She stopped at the table and grabbed the envelope.

You could hear her heart pounding so loudly that you would swear she was hooked to a heart monitor. She ripped open the envelope and out dropped a piece of paper with something written on it. As it fell to the floor, it seemed as if everything in the room was moving in slow motion. *What did I do?* All these crazy thoughts were now running through her head.

She closed her eyes, took a few deep breathes and calmed herself enough to pick up the paper. It had four words written on it, two on one line and two on the next. It read: ***LOOK WITHIN*** and ***BE CAREFUL.***

CHAPTER 13

There were mornings when you just wanted to pull the covers over your head and go back to sleep and this day was one of them. Five am came quickly when you go to bed late and the previous night was a late one. Griff had been going to his cycling class every Monday, Wednesday, and Friday, at 6am, for the past six years. Sometimes, on Tuesday and Thursday, he would join Abby for a morning walk. Since he had supposedly 'retired' he often found it difficult to get up and go to the gym. The verdict was still out on his capability to enjoy retirement.

Griff had been working since he was twelve years old. At a young age, his parents insisted he stayed busy with a job, or something to do. Griff didn't mind because he liked working and staying busy never felt like a chore. It made him the man he is today. One of the challenges he faced every day was making the rest of the world understand his 'Old School' ways. Often his work ethics were viewed as harsh in this day and age. Retirement was taxing for him to say the least.

With everything Abby's been enduring lately, he really wanted to join her that morning, but had an early meeting at the shop. Aside from still doing some work at the shop, Griff stayed busy managing all the rental properties they owned. There was always something to do whether it be insurance to pay or rent to collect. That particular morning, the insurance agent was coming by to talk about their current policies and how they could cut cost.

Driving to the shop, he thought about the events of the past few weeks. He could tell Abby was upset but he didn't know what to say or do to help her. From his perspective, she was definitely overreacting. She does tend to worry about things she has no control over. Even so, it bothered him to see her so upset. At least last night she appeared to be excited about the Halloween party and Harper being a part of it this year.

He was hoping to join Abby and Harper for lunch today, but time just got away from him. He realized he needed to spend more time with his youngest daughter, but the only thing they both enjoyed was going to dinner. Other than that, they don't have much in common. When Harper was a teenager, he would take her shopping on Magazine Street in New Orleans. He liked that Magazine Street was a charming little area of New Orleans filled with local vendors and restaurants. He would find a little café to sit and enjoy the afternoon, while Harper would shop the local stores. When she was finished, they would grab something to eat and head home. Occasionally, they would go to the movies. They still meet for dinner on occasion, but he feels like he's losing touch with her.

Abby made it a point to spend more time with Harper. She met her daughter for lunch each week and watched all the same shows in order to keep up with her. She always said that the teenage years were tough, and she was going to make sure she and Harper had common interest. It was important to Abby to be a part of her daughter's life. To be fair, they go shopping too, but Griff doesn't like to shop. Ever since Harper started driving, she drove herself and he could only stand watching 'World of Dance' so many times. It's definitely harder for fathers to find things in common with daughters.

Griff too was excited that Harper was interested in helping with the Halloween Party. He was hoping she would help him clean up and decorate. She's a really good worker if you could get her to find time to help. When she was little, she was always working with him, it didn't matter what he was doing. Abby always went all out decorating the house, so he hoped Harper had some ideas. He had planned on talking to her that night.

Since Abby had been on edge lately, Griff decided to head home early, but had to stop at the hardware store first. He forgot his phone in the truck, as usual, and when he came out of the store, he saw that Abby had called him several times. *This can't be good.* He tried to call her back, but it went straight to voice mail. She probably called Olivia since she couldn't reach him. He had to admit he was a little worried, which was not like him at all. All this craziness had begun to rub off on him.

He finally got home and noticed Olivia's car in the driveway. A little alarmed, he hurried into the house and found Abby sitting at the kitchen table, white as a ghost, with a piece of paper in her hand. Relieved that she was alright, he relaxed a little and waited for her to tell him what was going on.

After he listened to Abby explain everything that happened just before he arrived, he was speechless. He wasn't all that concerned before, but this was alarming. *What should we do? Should we call the police? The letter sounded harmless, but what if there was more to it. It was probably a prank, but who do we know that would do something like that?* One thing that stood out in Griff's mind was that man in the Dodge dart that Abby thought was following her. That's not a common car and the fact that she saw him twice did peak his concern. Not to mention, E.R. describing the same car stopping to help him with his tire. After talking to Abby a while longer, they decided to sleep on it and decide in the morning.

Griff's alarm clock started buzzing but, he decided he would hit the snooze button. With everything going on he had a restless night, partly because he was feeling a little guilty for thinking Abby was overacting. He loved his wife more than anything and would do whatever he had to in order to protect her.

Sometimes, when he looked at Abby, he wondered, *How did I got so lucky to have her, not only as my wife, but my best friend?* They are quite different, but they complement each other.

One of his favorite things about Abby was her most generous and forgiving heart. She was always upbeat and had a tenacious attitude that allowed her to accomplish the things she wanted most in life. With that said, she also had a big imagination and often went way overboard when planning something. She was a loving mother to their children and grandchildren, but most of all they were a team. They raised their kids and since then it was all about them, as it should be.

Griff started a "Bucket List" after his heart surgery in 2011 and since Harper had turned 20, Abby had more time and was working on making it happen. One of the first things on the list was going to Heinz Field in Pittsburgh, in the cold, at night, to see a Pittsburgh Steelers game. Abby had been researching and planning that trip for months. She bought short and long sleeve Steelers t-shirts for both of them. She wanted Griff to have the best experience he could. Those are the things he loved about his wife.

Now it seemed something strange was going on and it had Abby rattled all the time. It was time to do a little research and he knew just the guy to help, Tab Coulon, Griff's best friend since grade school.

Griff and Tab went to school together and stayed friends. After graduation, Tab went off to Louisiana State University (LSU) while Griff went to University of Southern Mississippi (USM). Tab lived in Baton Rouge for a while but moved back to the area a few years ago. They tried to get together at least once a week and go fishing but that didn't always work out. Tab worked at the District Attorney's office and stayed pretty busy. Since Griff 'retired' he was going to push Tab to get together more often because they weren't getting any younger. Griff decided he would go ahead and give Tab a call and ask him to lunch in order to get his perspective on things. Maybe he would at least be able to find out who owned the Dodge Dart and that would be a good start.

The alarm clock went off again and he contemplated getting up and attending his spinning class. It was clear that he wouldn't be able to fall back to sleep and it would do him good to burn up some energy and release stress. He was just worried about Abby, but as far as he knew she didn't have anything planned for the day and would probably end up sleeping in. He planned on being back by 7:30am and would be there to fix her breakfast and go over everything again with her.

After deciding to go to his class, he walked out the door to leave. Before he got in his car, he went to look around the porch and yard for anything that could help explain the envelope and who might have put it there. He really wasn't sure what he was looking for, but he walked all around checking the windows. Everything appeared to be untouched, but something felt odd. *Great,* he thought, *now I'm spooked, just like Abby.*

As he headed to the gym, he made a mental note to talk to the mailman about the envelope. He usually passed around 10am, but there was no way to be sure. Griff would have to be sure to keep an eye out in order to catch him. Maybe the mailman found the letter in the mailbox and wanted to bring that detail to their attention, but why would he ring the doorbell and leave? It was probably a long shot but worth looking into.

The gym was full when he arrived. It was crowded with everybody trying to get a jump on holiday eating. People think they can lose weight before the holidays so they can eat whatever they want during the holidays. It always amazed Griff how at different times of the year, more people joined the gym, attended a few weeks, and then quit until next time.

His spinning class had its regulars, but every now and then, someone new would attend and then you'd never see them again. It was a difficult class, which most people don't realize. Griff noticed before the class started that there was an older man in the back of the class. It *would be nice to have some more guys join*. Then man looked fit, but you don't know until class starts if someone had the endurance to keep up and finish. Most people in the class were women. There was only Griff and one other man who attended regularly and the conversation throughout the class was normally geared towards women.

Griff normally talked to everyone before class, especially new people, but today he was a little late to class and had just enough time to set up his bike. That was the one thing about this instructor; she was adamant about starting and ending on time. Some of the instructors at the gym were always late. The other thing Griff liked about this instructor was that she played good music. Being a little older than most of the others, he liked rock and roll. Once in a while, she played some 90's stuff, which Griff does not like, but it was not that often, so he did his best to put up with it. Today he was thankful that she played rock and roll because that helped get him through class.

After class ended, Griff got caught talking to the lady on the bike next to him and when he scanned the room for the new guy, he was already gone. He can't be sure when he left if it was right before or right after cool downs. It was common to have a lot of new people skip the cool down and rush out. Everyone else spent time chatting and gathering up their stuff, but Griff was anxious to get home to Abby, so he ran out as well.

As he was walking out the front door of the gym, he caught a glimpse of a car leaving the parking lot and it looked a lot like a Dodge Dart. He suddenly jumped into a sprint towards the car, stopping at the corner of the building, but he missed the car. He stood there, out of breath, mind racing and thought, *Ok – I'm sold. This is no longer a coincidence.*

CHAPTER 14

That morning, Abby slept in, and when she did finally wake up, it was a struggle to get out of bed. Without any restful sleep the previous night, her head was pounding and her stomach turning. The idea of someone leaving that note on her porch only made her realize that whoever left it, knew where she lived. She had never felt anything but peace at her home, and now she felt exposed, frightened, and as if she weren't already, this certainly made her a nervous wreck.

Griff went to work out at 6am that morning, and when she looked at the clock, she saw that it was nearly 8am, so he should have been home by now. *What if something has happened to him?* As her mind jumped from one unanswered question to the other, she focused on what felt like the worst part about all of this, which was, not knowing what that message meant. *Could it be someone from a church trying to get a message across?* It had been a long time since they had Jehovah's Witnesses come to the door. In Crown Point, the houses are spread out, not close like in neighborhoods so they would have had to drive from house to house. And sometimes they do leave literature on the door, but that envelope was blank.

With a jolt of energy, Abby jumped out of bed and looked to see if Griff was back and if Harper's car was home. Sometimes Harper slept out, but she always sent a text if she did. Thank God, both cars were home. Griff must have been in the kitchen and no doubt, Harper was still sleeping.

Abby dressed and headed down to the kitchen where Griff was busy making breakfast. He makes the best potato omelet, and that's exactly the smell coming from the kitchen. Abby was in the habit of skipping breakfast since the start of all the craziness, but as she smelled the omelet, her stomach began to growl. She was a comfort eater, so her will power faltered a little when she was nervous. It is amazing how food can make you feel so good. Griff always said she wanted 'instant gratification' and while he's probably right she didn't care. She's decided she would have a good breakfast then head off to get some answers.

"Good Morning." Griff kissed his wife's cheek.

"Good Morning Griff. It smells amazing in here. What's that you're cooking?"

"That would be my famous potato omelet. I know you love it and I wanted to cook breakfast for my beautiful wife this morning."

"Dad! What about me, dad? I thought you liked cooking breakfast for me," Harper said looking annoyed.

Abby, surprised to see her youngest daughter up before noon on her day off said, "Well good morning to you Harper. To what do we owe the pleasure of your presence at breakfast this morning? Not that it's not great to have both of you here, I'm just surprised."

"Dad woke me up earlier because he said he wanted us all here to discuss what's been going on lately. Mom, why didn't you tell me any of this before, I'm not a kid you know."

"No one said you were a kid. In fact, I didn't even tell your sister anything. At first, I thought I was overacting, but I think we're past that now. The events of the past month stood out as strange to me, but I couldn't figure out why. Little things, like the unexpected deaths of a few people I didn't even know, bothered me. The deaths indirectly affected me or someone I know, otherwise, I wouldn't have known about their deaths. And until the man in the Dodge Dart helped E.R. with his tire, I was hoping it was just a coincidence. I can't help feeling like this note has something to do with all of it, but I don't know what that would be." Abby realized she was shaking and walked over to the refrigerator to get a glass of juice and calm down. She didn't like her daughter or her husband seeing her this way.

Griff announced, "After breakfast I'm going to call Tab and see if he can help. I'm hoping he can tell us who owns the Dodge Dart, and then maybe we can track them down and get answers. I want both of you to keep your eyes and ears open, especially coming and going from home. Whoever put that note here may be watching us. And Harper, please answer your phone if we call. We don't want to worry if something has happened to you."

"Dad, I always answer my phone."

"No Harper, you don't always answer, but please be considerate of what your mother is going through and answer." Griff tried to keep calm with her, but that is the one thing that drives him crazy. That cell phone was never out of Harper's hands, unless she was eating with them, but only because they had a "no cell phone" rule at the table. Griff felt like everywhere they went, young people had their phones in their hands, and it made him sad to see how dependent kids are on technology.

"Harper, what are your plans for today?" Abby hoped she'd be staying home today.

"I asked Henley to go with me to the Halloween stores to look for our costumes for the party. I had a client today, but they cancelled, so, I thought, since I was off, I would start looking for something to wear. Mom, I already invited about 10 people, and everyone is excited. Henly and I will probably grab lunch, too. I'll check in, I promise. Thanks for breakfast, dad." And with that she got up from the table, kissed both Abby and Griff, and disappeared upstairs.

"How'd you manager to get her up early and in a good mood?"

Griff had that exact thought himself when he woke her up. She was usually cranky to say the least. "Food! I told her I was cooking breakfast and you know Harper and food. And I think she was already planning to get up to meet Henley. It was nice to have her here for breakfast, I miss her."

Griff took his wife in his arms and held her tight. He knew she was on edge and wanted to see her happy again. "It's going to be alright. I'm not going to let anything happen to you or the girls. What do you have planned for today?"

"I also wanted to go shopping. I thought about your suggestion for us to be Morgus and Chopsley and I like it. In fact, were going to decorate the house like a laboratory. What do you think?"

"I think you should stay home, or at least get Olivia to go with you. Abby, something is going on, and until we figure it out, we have to be on high alert. And wait until tonight to go for your walk, I'll go with you. I'm going to call Tab and then shower, but please promise me you'll be careful."

"I promise to be careful, but I will not let someone scare me into hiding out. Griff, yesterday, when I was walking, I kept hearing the sound of a car, but it never passed. I assumed it was on another street, but now I wonder if it was the person that left the note. Did he follow me home? There are so many unanswered questions. I'll wait to walk with you tonight and I'll call Olivia. I'll check in with you all day, deal?" Abby kissed her husband, thanked him for breakfast and began to clean up the kitchen.

Griff called Tab and scheduled lunch with him for 11:30am. They agreed to meet at a local restaurant called 'Da Wabbit' in Gretna. He knew Tab would suggest going there; it's his favorite place. They did have great food and it was close to Tab's office.

Before he forgot, Griff wanted to call someone to install cameras around the house. He knew it was too late to aid in the current set of circumstances, but it would provide extra security for the future. It was something he'd been thinking about and now wished he had acted on it earlier. He hoped the person that left the note never comes back, but if they do, he would be ready.

Griff arrived at the restaurant to meet Tab. He saw Tab's truck in the parking lot, so he knew he was already there. The sign read 'Home of Da Wabbitt.' This place had been here forever. When they were young, it was the local hangout, and Griff and Tab would grab hamburgers there with friends. A few years back, new owners opened it up and were again serving great food, which meant it was usually full, and hard to get a table.

Griff walked in and found Tab waiting at the bar. It was one of those restaurants where your entire party had to be present before they would seat you at a table. Tab was talking to a young man next to him, and when Griff walked up to them, Tab introduced the young man as Trey. Apparently, he works at the D.A.'s office with Tab. He was the son of another college buddy. He asked Griff if he would be comfortable with Trey joining them for lunch. He explained that Trey was new there and he was showing him the ropes. Normally, Griff liked to keep his business private, but if Tab liked the young man, then it was okay with him. Already, there was something about

Trey that Griff liked, and who knew what he could bring to the table to help solve Griff and Abby's dilemma. Having a young guy with technology skills could be an asset in this situation.

They enjoyed catching up for a while and getting to know the new kid. Trey had recently graduated college and was headed to law school but decided to take a year off. His parents were both attorneys and his whole life was geared that way. He had recently experienced doubt and his path was no longer clear cut for him. They sat discussing the pros and cons for a while. His favorite part of a case had always been the research. Trey was really interested in becoming a private detective, but he didn't want to disappoint his family. That was one of the things Griff liked about him already. He respected his family and their feelings. But Griff also always believed that you should follow your heart. Loving the job, you do made life so much nicer. Griff could relate to that, because he had always loved his job and was finding it difficult to retire.

"Well Trey, it sounds like you have some soul searching to do. Just remember to be true to yourself. I'm sure your parents love you and will understand. When my youngest daughter declared that she was not going to college, but instead to cosmetology school, we were upset for a moment, but then realized that was her passion and accepted her choice. I don't know if she cared as much as you do about what we thought. She's always been a very head strong independent girl and does what she wants to do." Griff smiled as he thought of Harper standing in the kitchen and not asking but telling them she was not going to college. He always knew she would find her own way and she had. They were proud of her and probably should tell her that more often.

"You should talk to your parents and give them a chance to understand," Griff added.

"I know they will, it's just that I don't like to disappoint them. Besides, working with Tab has given me the chance to see if this is what I really want to do. I have a year to figure things out, but thanks for the advice," he smiled at both Tab and Griff.

Tab smiled back, and then turned to his old friend and asked with concern, "So buddy, what's going on?"

Griff proceeded to tell them everything and, in the process, felt a little crazy.

"So, when this envelope appeared at my house yesterday things suddenly felt very real."

"Man, that would scare the heck out of me, too. What do you need me to do? We can research the Dodge Dart and see what we come up with. In fact, this would be right up your alley Trey. What do you think?" Tab turned to Trey for an answer.

"I don't know how much I can find, but I will definitely try. Do you have any other information on the car?" Trey asked eagerly.

"Not a lot. I had my wife look at some pictures on the internet and we determined that it is either a 1963 or 64' Dodge Dart and it was dark blue. It was in mint condition.

That's all we have at the moment. She did notice it was an older man, maybe in his 70's driving the car."

"That's actually a rather good start. There can't be that many old Dodge Darts running around these days. Do they still make that car?" Tab dabbled a little in cars and was familiar with that particular one. In fact, he never missed an event in Biloxi, Mississippi called *'Cruisin' The Coast.'* As luck would have it, it was happening the following weekend. The event draws tons of old and unique cars to the area each year. Since the suspect had an old car, he might just be there, and Tab wondered if they might get the chance to question to him.

"Trey's going to research online to find out what he can. Are we still on for this weekend for *Cruisin' The Coast*? Never know who'll show up there."

Griff felt rattled with uncertainty and said, "I'll let you know. With everything going on I hate to leave Abby alone, but I bet you're right. That Dodge Dart might be there. Let me see what I can work out and I'll call you later today. Thanks for all the help."

He called Abby's phone first and was relieved to hear her voice. She said Harper just called her, so that's also a relief. He told her he would be home soon. He was still feeling guilty that his wife had carried this load alone the past few weeks. *After we get some answers, we're going on a long weekend getaway to enjoy some much-needed relaxation,* he thought as he hung up the phone and began home.

CHAPTER 15

After dinner, Abby reminded Griff that they still needed to get that walk in. She grabbed the walking stick and a bottle of water, and they set off. It was a beautiful evening, and just being outside helped them both begin to relax. Griff grew up in Crown Point and had always loved the outdoors. When he was young, Crown Point was mostly farmland. Through the years, houses had gotten bigger and bigger and the area more populated. People wanted to live there because of its small-town country feel.

"I had lunch with Tab today and a young man he's working with joined us. They're going to try and find out who owns that Dodge Dart and hopefully get an address."

"That's great! Did they say how long it would take?"

"No, but I imagine it won't be long. That young man with Tab is on top of his game with the internet. I'm hoping to hear from them, if not tonight then tomorrow." Griff noticed his wife was still on edge, even after walking a few miles, which usually relaxed her mentally. She used to have anxiety attacks and had worked so hard to overcome them, that he hated to see her like this. She looked like she was one step away from panicking.

"I want to know everything they find on this guy. I know in my gut that he's been following me, and he needs to be held accountable for making me feel crazy." Abby felt her blood pressure rise the more she thought about it. "I bet he was the one who put that envelope on the porch too. He had better have a good reason because, as it stands now, I want him arrested for stalking."

"Abby, don't you think you're jumping the gun a bit? We don't know anything about this guy, and we surely don't know if he's following you. What happened to the liberal Abby, always a bleeding heart for everyone? What about innocent until proven guilty? I think you need to cool down a bit and wait until we have proof."

"I'm just sick of people in this world today who take every opportunity to make other people miserable. What happened to justice? There are so many bad people who never pay for what they do. Things need to change! Can we talk about something else? Did I tell you I found an old lab coat and a Morgus wig today? I had a nice time with Olivia, and we accomplished a lot for the Halloween party."

Just when Griff thought his wife was calming down, a car came barreling by speeding probably close to 70 miles an hour. Luckily, they were on the side of the street, and nothing was coming the other way. Usually people drove the speed limit in that neighborhood but once in a while, some idiot came by.

Abby lost it. She yelled at the top of her lungs and even picked up a rock and threw it at the car. Griff grabbed the walking stick before she could throw it at them.

She screamed, "I hope you have a blow-out you idiot!"

Griff didn't know what to say. Never in 20 years of marriage had he seen his wife act like that. Sure, she had road rage and was impatient like the rest of them, but never had she wished anything bad on anyone, not even people she didn't like.

They might have to take that little weekend vacation sooner than planned, but there's no way Abby would be willing to leave Harper at home. Not with everything going on and getting Harper to go out of town with her boring ol' parents would be impossible. But Griff was convinced that something had to happen, and soon.

After her walk, Abby went into her room to take a long bath and regroup. She kept candles all around the bathtub, but it had been forever since she used them. That night was just the perfect occasion to light them. After turning down the lights, Abby stayed in the tub for hours gathering her thoughts. Earlier, after the car passed, she saw in Griff's face that her behavior was out of control. She herself knew when she was yelling at the car, that it was inappropriate, but something inside was driving her on. For a moment, the anger felt good. It was as if she was not in control at all. She felt the anger bubble up from her core and demand to be released. She can't, in all her years, remember ever feeling like that before.

Closing her eyes, she whispered, *Get a grip Abby.*

She decided to practice the technique she used when she needed to gain control of her mind. Mindfulness, staying in the present and keeping your mind focused on that moment. That was what usually helped her get past the panic attacks she used to have. You would think it would be easy to stay focused on something, to control your mind, but Abby always found focusing on something and controlling her mind to be incredibly hard. It was a practice that took a long time, and she needed to really stay at it for it to work for her. She still had a long way to go to master the technique if that was even be possible.

As she sat in the tub, surrounded by candles, practicing her mindfulness, she finally felt the tension slowly leave her body, as if from one muscle at a time. She had used the candle flame to focus. At first, she stared at the candle and within the first minute her mind wandered 100 times to all the events of the day. As time passed, she was able to focus longer and longer. Soon, she fell asleep and didn't wake until Griff came in to check on her a few hours later.

It barely took 15 minutes before she was in her bed, and fast asleep. Griff checked on her a few more times before finally coming to bed himself. He was too wound up to go straight to sleep, so he tried to read for a while. After a few minutes, he gave up, because his mind was on Abby, and he couldn't think of anything else. He decided that the following day, he would suggest she schedule an appointment with her doctor and bring him up to speed. She needed to tell him what she has been dealing with and how she was handling it. Hopefully, her behavior was related to the medication she was on, and they could adjust it. He hoped.

Thankfully, Tab called first thing in the morning with some information. Apparently, there was a dark blue 1964 Dodge Dart registered to a man named Clay Hawkins from Summit, Mississippi. He was retired from the Brookhaven Police Department. Trey was able to get an address on the guy.

Tab asked if Griff was ready for a road trip. He and Trey were going to Summit to see what they can find out. They would be there in an hour to pick him up, so he had to tell Abby what was going on. He hated to wake her up. She looked so peaceful.

Just as he suspected, Abby wanted to go with them, but thankfully agreed that it would not be a good idea. He played the "Harper" card and she immediately realized if they both left town, Harper would be alone. Alex was always there for her, but with everything going on, Abby wanted to stay close to her children.

Please be careful and call me as soon as you get there,"

"You know how cell phone reception is hit or miss out there. I'm not sure how far from the interstate he lives or if he lives in the town of Summit. I'll try, but don't worry if you don't hear from me right away. It's 9am now and it takes about 2 1/2 hours to get there without traffic. If there is no reception you won't hear from me before 12:30pm at the earliest. I'll be with Tab, so don't worry; this is what he does. I have to go. I think I hear Tab driving up now. Love you." Griff kissed his wife and headed for the door.

Almost 3 hours later, Griff, Tab and Trey arrived at the house the car was registered to. The house was outside of town about 15 minutes and looked rundown and in need of repair. The grass was overgrown, and newspapers blanketed the driveway. The house was set back off the road, almost hidden with brush and trees that were also in need of some attention. As far as they could tell, there were no other houses around.

Tab parked on the street, a little away from the house. He knew from experience, that although the house looked disserted, it may not be. He was surprised to find the house in the shape it was in, and he was concerned about the type of person that would live there. Clay Hawkins was a retired detective and should have a decent pension. Tab's first instinct told him this was not going to be good. For an instant, he questioned his judgment on bringing Griff along, especially since they're not sure what they'd discover.

Before coming, Tab did his research. Det. Hawkins worked on a lot of murder cases through the years and retired in good standings with the Brookhaven Police Department. He was lead detective on most of those cases. He was never married, which could explain the condition of his house now. For the most part, on paper, he seemed like a normal guy, held in high regard with his colleagues. The only thing that stood out was his work on several cases that the detective concluded were related but happened over a span of 50 years. When Tab got back to his office, he had planned on expanding his search, with an emphasis on those cases. But for now, the task at hand was to find out if anyone was home and to determine what their interest in Abby could be.

Tab asked Griff to stay in the car, but that did not go over well. He did agree to stay back and let Tab and Trey go first. Griff couldn't help but think about horror movies he and Abby had seen. This house did look like it would be an excellent choice for one of those gory movies that had half breed humans killing and mutilating people, then cooking and eating them. Tab had never been a fan of horror movies either. Too often, the places he investigated looked like that and your mind could get away from you quickly if you let it.

He walked up to the front door while Trey went around the back. Griff stayed out by the road waiting for them to signal him that it was safe. This was the part of the job Tab loved heart pumping and senses on high alert. It was also the part where things could turn bad quickly. He noticed the mail piled up by the door, overflowing out of the mailbox. It was a solid door, no window, with a big red notice taped to it. It was a *Past Due - Disconnect Notice* from the electric company dated September 20, 2017. That was about 15 days prior.

Next, he backed off the porch to look in the picture window that was off to the right side. It presented a full view of the living room. The windows were cracked, covered with mildew and in need of immediate attention.

The whole house looked like it had been abandoned and left to rot. As far as Tab could see, there was no one home. He went back to the front door to knock. He turned the knob to see if it was locked and it was. Just then, he heard footsteps from inside the house coming towards the door and he sprang into action. Tab, with his gun in hand, stepped back and braced himself for what was to come. The door swung open and staring back at him was Trey.

Tab lowered his weapon and took a deep breath. He was not sure what he was expecting, but he was ready for anything. As much as he wanted to find this detective guy and get some answers, he was glad to see that it was Trey coming toward him.

Reading the look of surprise on Tab's face, Trey said, "The back door was wide open, and the screen door was barely hanging on. I heard you knock and waited to make sure it was empty. Man, I don't think anyone's been in here for a while. I tried the lights, but they don't work." Trey was filling in Tab while checking out the place.

"There was a disconnect notice on the door, so I figured as much. I'm guessing the back yard looks as bad as the front." Tab stepped inside.

The two of them searched the house starting with the room they walked into first, the living room. Aside from being terribly neglected, there was nothing out of the ordinary. The furniture looked like it was from the 1950's. They moved to the kitchen next which was surprisingly clean. Sure, it had dust and cobwebs everywhere and the furniture looked like it was old and outdated, but they were expecting dirty dishes and food all over the place. It seemed like someone gave up on this house long ago.

Tab heard footsteps coming up the porch and turned around to see Griff entering the house. They continued their search of the rest of the house. They turned the corner to the first room and realized, at that moment, they were definitely in the right house. Before Tab had time to process what he was looking at, Griff walked in behind them, and all three men turned white as ghost and were utterly shocked.

CHAPTER 16

SEPTEMBER 1987

As he moved across the house, Detective Clay Hawkins remembered having the same feeling in his gut a few years back. Something just didn't sit right with these murders. He was lead detective on two previous murder investigations that he was sure were related to this one. He happened to be in New Orleans visiting an old friend at the New Orleans Police Department when the call came in. He and NOPD Detective Rod Keller had been childhood friends and were getting together for lunch to catch up. The fact that he was there when this murder occurred told him it was no coincidence. He was just grateful that his friend invited him to go to the crime scene.

In the other two cases Detective Hawkins worked on, the people that were least likely to commit such gruesome acts were responsible for the murders. They were both upstanding citizens with no apparent motive. Also, everyone they interviewed had the same praise and admiration for each of them. Not one person had the slightest negative thing to say about the suspects. Usually, you can find 'that one person' who had a different view. The person that sees the darkness that everyone else fails to see. It was common for most people to have a few skeletons in their closet, but not the last two suspects. And if his hunch was correct, it would be the same thing for that woman sitting in the other room looking broken and devastated.

The thing that had stumped Detective Hawkins the most was the amount of time between the first murder case and the second one. The first was back in 1967 and the second wasn't until 1977, almost ten years later to the day. That had always haunted Detective Hawkins, and now, if this current murder in New Orleans was related, it will have been ten years since the last one. And with that, a definite pattern would emerge, but the significance of ten years was still a mystery. It was clear that it was not the same person that committed the crimes, so that ruled out serial killer. He knew there had to be a link, but he didn't know yet what it could be.

Walking through the crime scene, he continued to piece together facts from the other two cases with this one. The one different thing this time was that the person committing the crime was a woman. So far, he had been informed that this was her house, and the victim was her current boyfriend. She looked to be about sixty and was in excellent shape. She was an attractive woman and by the looks of the place, a very wealthy woman.

The house was in Audubon Place, a gated community in the high rent district of New Orleans. Just from the outside, Detective Hawkins guessed the house was at least 8000 square feet. He stepped inside to the foyer where a grand staircase stood that led upstairs to a loft and several bedrooms. His friend, Detective Rod Keller, informed him that there was also a library, a solarium and eight bedrooms. The backyard started with a covered slate patio that led out to a pool, a cabana, and beautifully landscaped grounds.

The lady of the house was a widow and had been dating the deceased for the past two years. His body, barely identifiable, was lying face down in the doorway between the kitchen and the great room. The victim looked to be in his sixty's as well and in decent shape himself. He was fully clothed except for shoes, he was barefoot. Detective Hawkins made a note of it and moved on. The amount of blood around the body led him to believe the attack took place where the body was laying lifeless. There was no one else in the house at the time of the attack, and the suspect appeared disorientated and distraught. She seemed to be overwhelmed with grief or maybe guilt and was having difficulty making sense when questioned.

The detectives called for a doctor to evaluate her and try to stabilize her enough to get a statement. Detective Keller also sent a few officers out to question the neighbors. He instructed them to get their opinions of the suspect. Again, Detective Hawkins felt confident that it would be just like the others; she was an upstanding citizen and well-liked by everyone.

They learned that her name was Roberta Baptist Shanely. Her late husband was a real estate mogul in New Orleans. He died a few years back and left her a fortune. There were no children from the marriage, and she had no relatives in New Orleans. Mrs. Shanely was originally from Brookhaven, Mississippi and still had family there.

Detective Hawkins was caught off guard when he heard that she was from Brookhaven, which was close to his hometown of Summit. He had spent years on the Brookhaven Police Department which meant he investigated crimes in a lot of the neighboring towns. The first two cases were local to the Brookhaven area, but this one occurred over two hours away in New Orleans. He didn't know what the connection was until he found out she was from Brookhaven.

Looking around, Detective Hawkins knew in his gut that this would be yet another case that kept him up at night and haunted his dreams.

CHAPTER 17

Walking into Ochsner Clinic to see her doctor, Abby found herself still on edge. She was lucky to get an appointment because it was usually hard to get in to see someone so quickly. She felt somewhat like a crazy person yelling after that car speeding down the street. Sure, she got mad, but that was a different feeling. It was a feeling of immense anger. And the way Griff had looked at her made her want to hide her face in shame. She'd been getting more and more angry and at the smallest things, which was very out of character for her. She was usually so easy going, even if she did live with anxiety at different points in her life. The obvious reason for the recent change in her behavior was stress, but her gut was telling her that it was something else.

Her mind was going a mile a minute, trying to understand what was going on and how to relay it to Dr. E. As she waited, she searched the web for causes of her sudden anger, personality changes and paranoia. *Brain Tumor, Schizophrenia, Head Trauma,* are just a few sites that popped up. *Well, I can rule out head trauma. And am I being paranoid? Maybe assuming the man in that Dodge Dart wasn't following me, but how do I explain the envelope left on the front porch?*

No, she agreed to come to the doctor to pacify Griff, but she was not crazy and doubted she had a brain tumor. And after receiving that envelope Griff looked scared, so she knew that he was beginning to feel concerned and worried that something was going on. He wouldn't have traveled to Summit with Tab had he not been worried.

Not hearing from Griff had her anxious and upset. It was only 11:30am, but she had hoped to hear something by now. What are the odds that this guy Griff, Tab, and Trey went to check on was the same person following her? Griff said that it was a rare car, but that still doesn't mean it was the guy. *Maybe the car was stolen,* Abby hypothesized but she was fairly certain Tab would have run a check on the plates before going all the way to Summit. She just had to be patient, and that did not come easy for her.

The nurse called her name to head back to see the doctor. She took a minute to gather herself, then set off to tell the doctor all the bizarre things that had been going on lately. She hoped he would believe everything she told him and that he wouldn't have her committed on the spot.

#

After securing the kitchen and living room, they signaled him to come in, which turned out to be a mistake. Griff was stunned when he turned the corner to meet Tab and Trey inside the house. Griff followed Tab into the room directly off the kitchen, which was empty of all furniture except a desk and a chair. The paint was peeling away from the walls and the floors were covered with a shag carpet that needed a good cleaning. The room was small and was probably used as an office at one time, but now, every inch, of every wall, was filled with photos and newspaper clippings from several murder cases. They were shocked by what they saw next. In the very center of one of the walls, in the middle of all the newspaper articles, thumb tacked to the wall was a large photograph. It was surrounded by a bunch of smaller ones, and they were all pictures of Griff's wife, Abby.

Griff's first instinct was to start ripping it all down. His mind raced with every horrible possible scenario he could think of. *What if I hadn't believed Abby and just ignored everything going on. It would have been easy to just pass it off as coincidence; that would have been my usual response.*

Why was this guy following Abby? What could possibly be the connection? We live almost three hours from this house. Griff noticed all the newspaper clippings and shuddered at the content of the articles and clippings. *Was this man responsible for all these other murders?* The walls were full of articles dating back to the 1960's.

Before he could say a word, Tab grabbed his arm and cautioned him not to touch anything.

"I know this is crazy man, but let's not disturb anything." Tab went on, "We'll take pictures of everything here so we can look over all of it later. We don't want anyone, especially the person this belongs to, to know we were here and are on to him. That might make him anxious and provoke him to do something that he may not be planning to do yet. I don't want to force his hand, not when Abby obviously has a part in his plan."

Griff stepped back. He knew Tab was right, but this had pushed all his panic buttons to the point of being terror stricken. In his entire life, he couldn't recall ever being that scared and feeling so helpless. It was overwhelming, and he suddenly felt like he needed to sit down. With his head shaking, he thought, *What a nightmare!*

Tab recognized the fear in his best friend's eyes and took a moment to make sure he was alright. "We're going to get this guy before he has a chance to do anything else. I already had Trey call in and have a police car park outside your house. You need to call Abby and make sure she's home without alarming her. Gather yourself and tell her that this place looked abandoned, so we decided to have your house watched in case someone tried to leave another note. Do not let on to what we found here."

Just about that time, Trey came back in the room and reported that a car was already in place in front of Griff and Abby's house. Trey then began to take pictures of the room, careful not to disturb anything. When they get back home, they were planning to examine the photos and see where they lead. They would also need to get a local detective to watch this house in case someone showed up.

Suddenly, all three men heard a sound at the back door. It was a faint knocking sound followed by that of a squeaky door. It sounded almost as if someone opened the door and entered the house. Both Tab and Trey sprang into action, guns raised, and moved towards the kitchen. The wind outside suddenly began to howl like a pack of wolves as the afternoon thunderstorms that were so common to the area began to roll in. Even though it's still daytime, the overcast outside caused the light in the house to dim, which made it difficult to see. Tab rounded the corner, with Trey on his heels, and stepped into the kitchen, towards the noise at the back door. To their relief, there was a cat sitting on top of the counter looking like he expected to be fed. They both relaxed and started laughing at the thought of a cat putting them on high alert. They were certainly on edge, and the laugh was much needed relief.

Griff gathered himself and decided to walk outside to call Abby. He was not sure if he had reception and figured it would probably be better outside. He dialed the house phone first with hopes that Abby was home and would pick up. If she was outside in the yard or on the patio, she may not hear it. While waiting for her to answer, he tried to figure out what to say. He was still clearly upset and prayed she didn't pick up anything too obvious in his voice. He wanted her to be safe, but he didn't want to alarm her.

Finally, she answered and was out of breath like she had been running. He figured this time of the day she was probably out on the patio.

"Hello, Griff is that you?"

"Hey Abs, I'm just checking in. We found the house, but no one was there. It looks abandoned and in need of a lot of work. We'll be heading back soon, and I'll fill you in. Tab put a car in front of the house, since Detective Hawkins is not here, just in case he shows up again. I just wanted you to know what's going on." Griff tried to sound calmer than he was and asked his wife, "Where's Harper?"

"She's spending the night at Henley's house. I spoke to her about an hour ago." Abby wondered why her husband's voice sounded odd. "Is everything alright Griff? You sound a little upset."

The lines on Griff's forehead were so pronounced that if she could have seen him, she would have known just how upset he was. Thankfully, he cleared his throat and was able to reassure her that it was nothing. They talked about her plans for the rest of the day, and he was relieved that she would be staying home. He told her he'd be home soon and as he hung up, Tab called out to him that they were finished here and ready to go.

Before they left, he did go back into the room and took a few pictures with his phone. This was one time he wished he had a better phone. Abby had been after him for years to get rid of his old flip phone to no avail. He didn't like all those buttons and different options on the new phones. With the flip phone, you could see who was calling and answer it, no fancy features. He did have to admit that lately he needed Abby to receive messages for him on her phone. Maybe it was time to upgrade and join the high-tech age.

#

The drive back seemed like it was taking forever. Griff sat there going over everything in his head. He felt like he was in one of Abby's horror movies she loved to watch. Tab and Trey were busy making phone calls trying to track this guy down. It sounded like he just disappeared off the face of the earth. He could hear the frustration in their voices after each phone call.

Before this trip, they were not sure if the man in the Dodge Dart had something to do with the envelope left on the porch. Now, it was definitely clear that he was following Abby and she had a part in whatever was going on.

Griff recalled the words in that envelope. 'Look Within and Be Careful.' What exactly could that mean? It sounded like someone was trying to send a warning not necessarily a threat. If that was the case, maybe this guy was not trying to hurt Abby. But what was the connection?

Griff didn't spend a lot of time reading the articles on the wall but did see enough to know that they were all about murders. The other thing that stood out to him was that they happened over a span of sixty years. Tab mentioned that this guy was a detective with the

Brookhaven Police Department. Was that his connection to the murders? It would explain the walls of pictures and articles. Did he find a connection between the murders?

"Trey, can you print out the pictures you took of the wall and get them to me? I want to look over them as well." Griff smiled a little, already really liking the new guy. "I really appreciate you coming along today. I know how busy you both are, so I just wanted to say thanks."

Trey, still looking at his phone nodded and said, "No problem. I'm glad I could help. It was the first time I was able to participate in an investigation, even if it wasn't official. I always thought this is what I wanted to do and today just confirmed that for me. So, I guess I should be thanking you man. I just hope we can find this guy soon."

"So, what's our next move?" Griff asked eagerly.

"Well Griff, if we can't find something on him by tomorrow, I say we head to Biloxi this weekend to *Crusin' The Coast*. It's just our luck he drives a rare car, so he may show up. Do you think you could call your buddy Pete and get us some tickets? And man, you don't have to come. I understand if you want to stay with Abby," Tab added, worried about his friend.

Griff, feeling a little better, was glad to have Tab for a best friend. They may not have seen each other all that much, but Tab always came through when Griff needed him, and he needed him now. "I'll let you know after I talk to Abby. I'll make a phone call and get those tickets. Trey, are you coming too?"

Trey smiled at the thought of going to *Crusin' The Coast*. He always wanted to go, but never had the chance. And he really liked both Tab and Griff. He had more in common with them than with most people his own age. A few days in Biloxi with old cars everywhere sounded like a perfect time to him.

Trey attempted to contain his excitement but failed miserably. "Absolutely! Count me in. What time do we leave? Are we staying overnight?"

Tab realized how excited Trey was, laughed and said, "Let's back up here a minute. Griff let us know if you can go as soon as you talk to Abby. Let's plan to leave around 6am to beat the traffic. We can decide later if we need to stay the night. I doubt there's a hotel available anywhere on the coast. I know a few people who have rooms already. If we need to, I'm sure we can crash with them. Bring an overnight bag just in case."

The ride the rest of the way home was quiet with everyone left to their own thoughts. They all knew the man they were looking for would not be easy to find. *Cruisin' The Coast* was like one big Block Party, with people everywhere. They could spend all day and possibly never cross paths with him. It wouldn't be hard to spot the Dodge dart, but they would have to be at the right place at the right time. But it was the best shot they had at finding him.

Griff was trying to decide if he should leave Abby home or ask her to go. She would probably jump at the chance to go to the *Golden Nugget Casino* for the weekend. He would be more at ease with her close by and in the casino full of people. It always amazed him the amount of people day or night in the casinos.

He tried to close his eyes and relax for a while. He knew the next few days would be hectic, and he needed all the rest he could get. He knew the weekend ahead would be an interesting one, for sure.

CHAPTER 18

Feeling better after talking to her doctor, Abby decided to call Olivia for lunch. They agreed to meet at Abby's for 1:00pm. With everything going on she didn't want to be home alone. Harper wasn't due home until the next day, at the earliest. Sometimes she stayed at Henley's all weekend.

She hadn't heard from Griff yet and that had her feeling anxious, which seemed to be her constant state of mind. Her doctor's appointment was quick, and she made it home before 12:30pm. She decided to relax a little and wait on Olivia. With the weather so nice outside, she sat out on the patio for a while.

Just when she was closing her eyes for a nap, the phone rang, and she had to run to catch it in case it was Griff. He usually called on her cell phone, but just in case, she ran inside to catch the phone. She noticed the caller ID and it was Griff. Relieved, she picked up the phone.

After their conversation, Abby went back to the patio and went over in her mind everything Griff said. He sounded tense, and that was not normal for him. He said everything was fine, but she knew her husband, and he was definitely keeping something from her, but what? He said the house was empty. And he said there would be a police car outside her house, but why would they feel the need to do that if everything was okay. No, she knew something was up and was glad Olivia was on her way.

She walked to the front door and looked out to the street. She couldn't see anything through the glass, so she opened the door. Parked in front of her neighbor's house across the road was a black car with tinted windows. She wondered if that was the officer watching her house. She thought it was going to be a squad car, not a plain car. Now she wished Griff would have specified that when they spoke earlier. What if someone else was in that car watching her.

She quickly went back in the house and locked the door. She hated how paranoid she had been lately, but better safe than sorry. She went to the front window and tried to see if she could make out anything on the car that would indicate that it was the police. It was too far away to see the license plate. It looked like someone was in the car, but the windows were so dark it was hard to tell for sure.

She decided to go call Griff and ask him what kind of car it should be. Right before she turned from the window a hand touched her shoulder. Abby screamed and turned ready to attack whoever it was and run. She leaped forward onto the person and at that moment realized it was Olivia, but it was already too late to stop, and they both tumbled to the ground.

They laid there stunned for a minute and then Olivia busted out laughing. Abby joined her and they laid there laughing for what seemed like forever. It couldn't have been too long because they suddenly realized that the doorbell was ringing, and someone had been banging on the door. It was a uniformed policeman, so Abby cracked the door and asked for his credentials.

He showed Abby his badge and said he heard a scream and wanted to know if everything was alright. That made Olivia and Abby burst into laughter again. She apologized to him and said that Olivia had startled her, but everything was alright. He went on to tell her that he was in fact placed there by Tab, and someone would be stationed out there around the clock.

She thanked him and shut the door. After another round of the giggles, they went to the kitchen to get some lunch. Olivia said that she parked in the back, as she always did, and called out for Abby. She thought Abby heard her and didn't realize that touching her arm was going to startle her like that. Abby figured she was probably so preoccupied by the car outside that she somehow missed Olivia pulling in. She must have arrived between the time she shut the door and walked over to the window. What were the odds of that?

Oh well, Abby thought. *At least I have my answer to who was in that car across the street.* That was how things went when you're on edge. It seemed like every little thing was turning into something crazy. Olivia always came through the back door and called her name when she came over. So much for Dr. E's advice, to take it easy and avoid stressful situations. He told her that under no circumstances should she and Olivia do any more investigating in a secluded area like a cemetery. That did sound a little crazy when she thought about it. She intended to take his advice and stay close to home for a while. Besides, Olivia was a wiz at Google, and they could do some research right there at home.

Griff didn't get back to the Westbank of New Orleans, until about 6 pm. The traffic was backed up on the Crescent City Connection, as usual. They left Summit around 1pm, and the traffic was light until they hit New Orleans. They thought about stopping to get something to eat but decided to drive straight through. Often, when he and Abby went to their camp in Magnolia, Mississippi, they would stop in Hammond, which was about halfway. It broke up the trip a bit and at their age, they liked to get out and stretch. Hammond had a bunch of restaurants to choose from. It's not New Orleans, but it did have some good choices. Aside from Hammond, most of the towns on the way to Magnolia were small and only have a few fast-food restaurants and maybe one mom and pop place. But on this drive back, they were all just ready to get home.

Griff called Abby and she told him Olivia would stay until he got home. That information made him feel a little better, but he was still so tense and worried. He needed to decide if he was going to Biloxi or not. It all depended on Abby and what she wanted him to do. If Harper was staying with Henly this weekend Abby might just go. Alex and Finn were likely to be home if Harper needed something, and hopefully whoever left the note on the porch was only watching the house. Biloxi was only about an hour and forty-five minutes away from home. He wouldn't leave his wife alone with all that was going on, so if she didn't want to go, he wouldn't go either.

Every time he closed his eyes and tried to relax during the drive home, he saw that wall with Abby's pictures in the middle. One thing that haunted him was how Detective Hawkins got all those photographs. *Did he follow her and take them himself? Did he get them off social media?* Facebook was so popular; everyone posted pictures all the time. It was a great way to share with friends and family, but sadly there were always ways to hack anything. And Facebook was not the only social media out there. There was Instagram, Snapchat, and Twitter, to name a few. Griff knew if he was familiar with those few, there were probably tons of other sites he had no idea existed. He was definitely not technologically savvy. Now, Abby was a bit more up to date on those things because of Harper. She used to have whatever social media Harper was accessing so she could monitor what she was doing, but Griff was sure Harper left Abby behind. He decided he was not going to tell Abby about the wall of photograph's they found in Detective Hawkins house. He wanted a bit more information before he told her, so he could get a better understanding of what they were dealing with. He broke out in a cold sweat and was rattled with all this uncertainty.

As he approached his house, he saw the car parked across the street. He wasn't sure if he should go talk to them or not. He decided not to and turned down the driveway. He noticed Olivia's car and pulled under the carport. She had proven to be a good friend over and over again. They tended to get themselves into crazy, odd circumstances, that most normal people never do. Luckily, it had always been harmless, and they end up having the time of their lives. They had been inseparable since school, and he knew that they would be that way for the rest of their lives. Griff was grateful Abby had Olivia and wouldn't have wanted it any other way.

He walked into the kitchen and there was no one there. He figured they must be upstairs in her craft room. Griff walked into the living room and the television was on. He missed the national news but decided to catch up on the local news. There was a news report of an accident that happened by their house, on the Lafitte Larose Highway around 7pm last night. Apparently, a car traveling at a high speed, lost control and flipped. The driver was in West Jefferson hospital in critical condition. An investigation was underway to determine what caused the car to flip.

Griff made a mental note to go back and watch the rebroadcast of the news later to see what he missed. All he could think of was Abby screaming at that car yesterday and wishing him harm. He heard Abby coming down and turned off the television. He was not sure why, but he had an uneasy feeling about what he had just heard. If it caused him alarm, it would definitely upset Abby.

Griff walked up to his wife and kissed her hello. He gave Olivia a hug and they all walked into the kitchen.

Griff looked at his wife and said, "So, how was your day?"

Abby and Olivia giggled and proceeded to tell Griff about the incident earlier. They were happy neither of them got hurt when Abby tackled Olivia.

"I wish I were here to see that. I bet you were surprised Olivia?"

Still giggling Olivia said, "I think we were both surprised. I really thought she heard me call her name and was just looking at something through the window. From now on, I'll make sure to be loud and clear when I walk into this house."

"Oh, don't be so dramatic Liv. You're just lucky I realized it was you when I did, we both are." Abby smiled and Griff was delighted to see that. It had been a while since he had seen her relax, much less smile.

"I'll fill you in about the trip to Summit today, but first I need to know if you want to go to Biloxi tomorrow for *Cruisin' The Coast*. Tab wants to go see if we can track down that Dodge Dart. I know it's a long shot, but you never know. We could stay at the *Golden Nugget*."

"I don't know Griff. Do you think we should go?" Abby had a concerned look on her face again. "And are you going to go with Tab to the Coliseum or stay with me at the casino?"

"Well, I probably will go with them for a while. The more eyes out there, the better. Even though that's not a popular car, there will be cars everywhere. We could miss him all together."

You can almost see the wheels turning in Abby's mind when she announced, "I have an idea. Olivia what are you and Jack doing this weekend?"

Being the friend she is, Olivia said, "My guess is that we're going to the *Golden Nugget* with y'all."

At that they all laughed.

CHAPTER 19

Interstate 10 East was slow moving when they hit the road to Biloxi. They left early in an attempt to avoid traffic. It was smooth sailing until they hit Mississippi and then it was flowing, but at a slower speed. It was when they hit the Gulfport exit that everything seemed to bottleneck. It was stop and go, bumper to bumper traffic. They had about three more miles to get to the next exit, and it was taking forever. Normally, they take the Biloxi exit off the interstate but today, with all the traffic, they decided to get off earlier.

Abby had fallen asleep in the car right after they left home. She tossed and turned like her usual fidgety sleep. When she finally woke up, they were almost to Gulfport. She knew Griff hated to drive anytime, much less in bumper-to-bumper traffic. She was hungry and needed the restroom, so she spoke up.

"Can we stop for something to eat? I could use a restroom break too."

"Yeah, we will if we can ever get to the next exit. We've been sitting here for over an hour now. Something must have happened because this is not usual morning traffic." Griff smiled at his wife who finally looked a little rested. "How was your nap? I know you were sleeping well because you were snoring so loud the people in the other car could hear you."

Abby laughed. Griff was always making some silly jokes about everything. She was glad to see him a little more relaxed this morning. Yesterday, he was trying hard to act like everything was alright, but she could tell he was a bundle of nerves.

"You are so stupid! I was not snoring, because I was not sleeping. I just had my eyes closed for a while." Abby grinned knowing full well she was sleeping and probably snoring.

Griff rolled down Abby's window and was gesturing the car next to them to do the same.

"Hey man, did you hear a loud sound like someone was..."

Before he could finish, Abby reached over and slapped him on the shoulder. Luckily, the people next to them wasn't even paying attention. He did that all the time. The kids used to get a kick out of it, but not Abby. It got old after years and years of it.

"Why are you so stupid all the time? Can you please get me to a bathroom?"

"What would you like me to do? Can't you see that we're not moving? And you called me stupid." Griff looked out his window so she couldn't see the smirk on his face. He loved aggravating her, and he knew it drove her crazy.

Finally, they reached the Gulfport exit and decided to stop and get breakfast. Olivia and Jack weren't meeting them until that evening and Tab and Trey were already there, so they were in no rush. He did have to meet up with his friend Pete to get the tickets for the car auction. He was glad he was able to get four tickets. They were weekend passes, so they should be able to come and go as they please. He had asked Pete if a Dodge Dart was registered for the auction, but as he figured, it was not. So, that meant that if Detective Hawkins intended to come, he would be a spectator. That would likely make him a little harder to find, but not impossible.

Abby called the *Golden Nugget* last night and was able to book two rooms. Normally, they are booked solid, especially with *Cruisin' The Coast* going on, but there was a last-minute cancellation at the same time she called. Maybe that was a sign that they would have good luck this weekend at the casino and finding their mystery man.

After breakfast, they headed to Biloxi. The traffic had cleared up and was moving at the normal speed. As expected, the closer you got to the Coliseum the slower the traffic was moving. It was amazing to see all the old cars rolling up and down the highway. There were people of all ages just trying to get a place to park and watch the unique cars pass by.

They stopped at a red light and a 1966 pale yellow Pontiac LeMans pulled up next to them, Abby's dream car. Once, a long time ago, they were up the East Coast in Maine and almost bought one. She decided she did not really want another car, so they walked away from it. Griff secretly thought she wished they had bought it. And by the look in her eyes now, he knew he was right.

"Griff look what's next to us. I was hoping we would see one, but I didn't really think we would." Abby was staring at her dream car and Griff didn't need to see her face to know she was smiling from ear to ear.

"Are you sorry we didn't buy the one we saw in Maine? I know you really loved that car."

"I did love it, but I'm not sorry. We have so much going on all the time, when would we have time to enjoy it. Besides, you have the 57 Chevy and I know you love it. We don't need two cars we never use. But it is really awesome seeing one again, and the same color. Do you think it could be the same car?" Abby continued to look at the car when her phone rang.

"Is that Harper? I recognize that ring tone."

"Yes. I wonder what she wants. She is never up this early unless she has work." Abby's stomach dropped for a minute before answering the phone.

"Good morning, Harper. What are you doing up this early?"

"Good morning to you, mom. I have a client in a little while and I have to get to the mall and pick up something first. Where are you?"

"Dad and I are headed to the *Golden Nugget* for the weekend. I was going to call you later to tell you, because I didn't want to wake you up. Where are you? I thought you were staying at Henly's this weekend." Abby was a little concerned her daughter decided to go to the house.

"I'm still at Henly's. I just called to see if you could have lunch today. I wanted to go back to Fuji Hanna's."

Abby smiled, "Are you hoping to run into that young man again?"

Feeling irritated Harper said, "Mom, what are you talking about? I just wanted to see if you were available. Besides, I already ran into him again."

"Really, so are you seeing him now?"

"We're talking if that's what you mean. He had to go out of town for work yesterday and we were supposed to get together tonight. He just texted me to say he had to cancel and go out of town again for work. In fact, he had to go to *Cruisin' the Coast* with his boss. Is that what dads there for? I know he usually goes with Mr. Tab every year. How did you get to go with them, isn't it usually 'guys' weekend?" Harper knew how to push Abby's buttons and she enjoyed it.

"First off, it's never been a 'guys' weekend. It just happened to be all guys the last few years. And Ms. Olivia and Mr. Jack are joining us. Dad and Mr. Jack are meeting Mr. Tab there later. Well I guess you realize I can't have lunch today. Sorry honey. What about Henly? Please remember, do not go anywhere by yourself right now. We still don't know who put that note on the porch or why. Promise me you will be careful. And Harper, I hope you get to go out with Noah. I saw the way you looked at him, and I think he feels the same way. Be patient okay." Abby could picture Harper rolling her eyes.

"Mom, I know. He said he would call when he gets back in town. He wasn't sure if they were staying Saturday night too. I guess it depends on his boss. I think I'm going to invite him to the Halloween Party." Harper was hoping her mother got the hint that she did not want to talk to her about her love life, by her changing the subject.

"Harper, why don't you and Henly come to Biloxi? You can spend the day by the pool and maybe get to see Noah later tonight. Surely, he's not working around the clock."

"Right and make him think I'm following him. I don't want to do that, but I do love the H2O pool at the *Golden Nugget*. I'll talk to Henly and let you know. I gotta go. I'll call later and let you know if we're coming. Love ya."

When Abby hung up, Griff noticed that he could see the match making look in Abby's eyes. She was so obsessed with Harper finding a boyfriend. He didn't understand why because she looked to be happy on her own these days. But he knew Abby's wheels were turning, and she was not going to stop. She always got on a roll when she had something like this to keep her occupied. You can tell she loved it and that made him happy to see her smiling, even if Harper wouldn't be. She was just going to have to take one for the team because Abby needed this right now.

CHAPTER 20

Harper talked to Henly, and they decided to go to Biloxi to meet her parents. It wasn't often she didn't have clients booked late into the evening on a Friday, so she figured it was a good time to go. Besides, she and Henly loved hanging by the pool. She called Abby and told her they were leaving later that night, after her last client and should be there around nine.

Harper needed to decide if she should text Noah and tell him or not. She didn't want him to think she was following him. She decided to wait until he texted her again, and then she would just tell him the truth, which was that her parents asked her to go. They don't have to meet up, but if he's free maybe they will. She and Henly will definitely go out either way. There's only one problem. Later tonight, before they leave, Harper had to go to her house to pack for the trip. She was not going to tell her mom, but she would wait for Henly to go with her.

It wasn't as easy as she thought it would be to convince Henly to go to her house with her. Her best friend was always scary about things and never did like to go to her house when her parents weren't home. She always tried to say no, but eventually let Harper have her way. That night was no exception.

Harper had stayed home alone a million times recently since her parents were always on the go. Driving down the driveway, she had an odd feeling come over her. From the street, the house looked dark and quiet and a little spooky. She could tell Henly felt it too by the look on her face.

"Tell me why we have to come here tonight? Your house is always spooky looking, but tonight it looks even more terrifying." Henly looked like she was going to jump out her skin any minute.

"Don't be ridiculous. I stay here all the time by myself, and you used to stay with me a lot of those times. What's the problem? I just have to run in and grab my bathing suit and a few things I need. It'll just take a minute. Do you want to stay in the car?" Harper said with a smirk knowing full well Henly would never stay in the car alone.

"Are you crazy? I'm going wherever you're going. Just hurry up. I thought you promised your mom you wouldn't come to the house. She's going to kill you if she finds out." Henly was right on her heels.

They turned off the alarm and headed up to Harper's room. She wasn't sure what to pack because she didn't know if they were staying until Sunday or coming home Saturday night. She laughed at herself because she knew she would pack way too much either way.

"Henly, can you grab my flat iron from the downstairs bathroom please?"

"No. I'm not leaving your side. Something doesn't feel right tonight, and that's your fault. Maybe if you wouldn't have insisted that I watch all those horror movies with you I wouldn't be as scared, but I am not going anywhere without you." Henly plopped down on Harper's bed and waited for her to finish.

Harper, looking aggravated with Henly, headed towards the stairs to go get it herself, but she stopped at the top and held her breath. She thought she heard a noise coming from downstairs. She turned to go tell Henly only to find she was right behind her. They stayed still for what seemed like forever and listened to see if she actually heard something or imagined it. She blamed Henly for her being on edge because she knew the house made all sorts of sounds in the night, and it was probably nothing. They walked slowly down the stairs to the half landing hoping to tell where the noise came from. From there they could see out of the picture window to the back porch. It looked like the back door was not closed all the way.

Harper whispered, "Did you not shut the door all the way and lock it like I said?"

"I did. I even checked the knob to make sure. Do you think someone is in the house?" Henly's voice trembled, "Oh my God! Do you have your phone on you?"

"No, it's in my room. Let's go back up but be quiet. Go slow because the stairs make noise."

They headed back to Harpers room and tried to figure out what to do next. She hated to call 911 if she was just imagining things. But Henly was sure she locked the door. Maybe she could call her sister Alex and see if it could be her by some chance. She dialed Alex but it went straight to voicemail. That was about right, when she needed her sister the most, she didn't answer her phone. What if it was someone here to burglarize the house? Both of her parents' cars were not home, only Harper's. Did they think the house was empty? The two of them didn't hear any more noise, and they started to think they were imagining things. Henly was a bundle of nerves when they got there so she probably just forgot to close the door.

"I'm going down to see what's going on. Stay here and be ready to call 911."

"No way! You're not leaving me here by myself." She grabbed one of Harper's old bats from when she played softball. They both grabbed their phones and put them on silent. That was all they need was the phone to ring when they were trying to be quiet. Harper thought, *Great, Alex will probably call me back as soon as she realized I called.*

They slowly walked out Harper's room and headed for the stairs. They paused with each step to listen carefully for any indication that someone was in the house. All was quiet so they continued. Harper stopped suddenly and Henly ran right into the back of her.

"What's wrong? Did you hear something again?"

"I thought I saw a shadow pass in the kitchen. It's hard to tell, but it looks like a person." Now Harper was scared. Before she was a little on edge, but she thought she was imagining things. What should they do if someone was in the house? They had reached the bottom of the stairs and could probably make it out the front door. But Harper's house was a long way from the road. They could run to the neighbor's house and hope that they were home. Why didn't they grab the car keys? Harper wondered if they should go back up and get them. If she had dialed 911 right then, if someone were in the house, they would have heard her.

Harper, feeling out of control, took a few deep breaths and tried to get a grip. *Think Harper! What would dad tell you to do?* She looked at Henly for some help, but she was barely holding it together.

"Okay Hen, at the count of 3 we are going to run out the front door and head next door. Do not stop and run as fast as you can. If they're not home, run to the road. Once we are out of the house and safe, I'm going to call 911. I'm afraid if I call now, they will hear me, and we won't be able to get out the house fast enough. Are you ready?"

Henly didn't say a word. She just barely nodded in agreement. She knew this was a bad idea from the start. Things have been too crazy lately.

"One, two, three!" On three, Harper grabbed the front door handle, flung open the door and they both ran for their lives. Neither one stopped or even looked back until they reached the neighbor's house. Of course, the neighbor's house was in total darkness, which meant no one was home.

They both crouched down on the side of the garage and looked back at the house. Henly dialed 911 while Harper looked back towards the house to see if anyone saw them. Harper's stomach dropped as she saw a man running from her house. He was running to the back yard towards the bayou. *Is he going into the woods?* Henly said the police were on their way. They weren't sure if they should head to the road or just stay put. One thing was for sure, her mother was going to kill her.

The police arrived, and even though it seemed like forever, they were there in 7 minutes. They began to search the house and the backyard. There was no sign of anyone anywhere. There were no signs of forced entry. In fact, there was no evidence of anyone being in the house. Suddenly, Harper remembered the cameras around the house and told the police about them. They went inside so she could look at the cameras.

It took her a few minutes to remember how to work the system. Her mother was usually the one who operated it, never her. The only reason she knew the password was from watching her mother a few times. Finally, she figured it out and began a search for today's date. She sat there, stunned watching what had just happened.

#

Earlier in the day, after Abby had set up the plan on the phone with Harper, Griff and Abby finally arrived and got checked into the *Golden Nugget.* They were able to book another room for Harper and Henly. Harper always took forever to get ready for anything, so it was better for her to have her own room

They decided to take a little time in the room and relax a bit. They both liked to play at the casino, but they tried to pace themselves, especially if they were staying for a few days. You could lose a lot of money quickly if you weren't careful. Just breaking even after a weekend in Biloxi was all they hoped for. They both fell asleep and didn't wake up until Griff's phone rang a few hours later.

Griff whispered, trying not to wake up Abby. "Tab, what's up man?"

"Nothing man, just checking in. We're heading back to the coliseum to see what's going on. Do you want us to pick you up?"

Griff noticed it was already 1:30pm. "Yeah, give me about 20 minutes and I'll meet you downstairs."

He couldn't believe they had slept that long. And Abby was still sleeping. He wrote her a note and left a few hundred dollars on the dresser just in case she wanted to go gamble a bit. She liked being out by the pool too, especially when it was not so hot. But the way she was snoring right now, she may sleep the rest of the afternoon. He guessed being away from all the mess allowed her to relax; it sure did for Griff. If his phone hadn't rang, he probably would've still been sleeping.

He dressed and left the room as quietly as possible so he wouldn't wake up Abby. The guys were waiting for him downstairs when he got there. Again, the traffic going to the coliseum was bumper to bumper. It was only going to get worse as the day continued. Especially after 5 o'clock when everyone got off work for the weekend.

Trey suggested parking in front of the coliseum on Beach Road, so they could watch all the cars pass by. Most people coming for the auction or the car show at one point or another passed in front of there. They found a place to pull over and hang out a while. It was not too bad waiting this way because it was really cool to see all the cars. Griff had never been on a stakeout, but always figured they would be long and boring. Not this one. They stopped and picked up some beer before they parked, knowing they were going to be there a while.

"We need to talk about what to do if we see that Dodge Dart. We don't want to let on that we know who he is and that we are looking for him. He may run and we'll never find him." Tab drank his beer sitting on the tailgate of his truck. "With this traffic he wouldn't be able to get away in the car, but he could leave it if he thought he had to."

Griff didn't know how to respond to that. Of course he wanted to get this guy, but he knew what Tab was saying was true. "Whatever you guys think, I'm just along for the ride. Both of you know a hell of a lot more than I do about this stuff. Tell me what to do and I'll do it. We just really need to talk to this guy soon."

"Traffic is almost at a crawl. I say, if we see the car, maybe we can follow it on foot for a while. Trying to get the truck out would not be fast enough. I don't think we should try to stop him unless he is at a dead stop, and we have time to surround the car. We'll have to make that call if he even passes here. The odds are we won't see him at all this weekend."

Griff knew Tab was right about that too, but he prayed he would come out and they got a chance to talk to him.

CHAPTER 21

Harper's whole body was full of goose bumps. It was chilling just how close they came to running into this guy breaking into her house. As she watched the footage from the cameras, she started to tremble and became sick to her stomach. Henly watched for a few minutes, but it became too much for her to handle. Harper shuddered at the thought of what would have happened if he hadn't heard them drive up. Things could have turned out a lot worse for them.

Around 8:15, a man wearing a black hoodie, black pants, and gloves, came into the view of the camera that faced the bayou at the back of the garage. He never looked up, so you can't see his face. It's as if he knew the cameras were there. He proceeded to walk close to the garage where it was darkest until he got to the carport. It was just dark enough to give him protection. He went to the sink by the garage door and retrieved the spare key hidden behind it.

Harper let out a gasp. *How did he know that was there? Could it be someone we know?* She paused the tape to gather herself again. The horror unfolding in front of her eyes was difficult to watch. She'd always felt so safe in Crown Point. During the day, they left the back door open, and the screen door unlocked. They didn't even lock their cars at night. They always tried to keep the location of the extra keys hidden a secret. Her dad was very adamant about that and changed places often.

She gathered herself and hit play again. She would love to just get in her car and head to Biloxi with her parents, but she felt a need to watch the actual events unfold.

He then went to the back porch and opened the door. He went to the alarm panel and punched in the code. At that very moment, the camera on the front of the carport picked up a car coming down the driveway. The car came all the way under the carport, parked and she and Henly got out. He hurried to put the alarm back on, and then you could see from the patio camera, that he headed through the kitchen towards the hall. *This is unbelievable. How did he know the code and where to hide in my house?* They enter the house and Henly did shut and lock the door. At that point, they were locked in with the intruder.

Harper paused the tape again and walked outside where Henly was sitting for some fresh air.

"Did they find anything yet?"

Harper was glad to see her friend had calmed down. There were policemen everywhere looking for this guy. They figured he was long gone but continued to search for clues. She knew she'd better call her dad, but she hated to upset him. There was nothing he could do now. Maybe she should call Mr. Tab first and let him tell her dad.

She decided to go inside and finish watching the recording from the cameras, then, she and Henly were going to get on the road. She'll call her parents then, because it was already going to be way later then 9pm when she got there.

She went back to the computer and pressed play on the DVR one more time. Everything was quiet and dark for a few minutes, then you see the intruder trying to quietly open the back door. That must be when Harper thought she saw a shadow downstairs. Next, the camera in the front of the house showed Harper and Henly running out the front door, and the patio camera showed a man running out of the back of the house towards the bayou.

It appeared they arrived at her house just when he got there and spooked him. Harper sat back to take it all in. She felt violated like someone was in her space. Victimized would be a better word. She was reminded of those commercials on television of people who were robbed, and how they said they felt so helpless. Now, she understood exactly how they felt, and she was not happy about it.

The police wrapped up the search and informed her that it appeared the intruder was long gone. He also told her they contacted Tab, and he ordered a car to be there around the clock just in case. Earlier, he took off the detail on Harper's house he had for the weekend, since no one was going to be home. Harper jumped when her phone rang.

"Harper this is Mr. Tab. Are you alright? I just spoke to the officer there and he brought me up to speed. Did you call your parents yet?" Mr. Tab sounded worried.

"Yes, we're okay, just a little rattled. We're getting ready to head that way as soon as the police are finished up here. I didn't call my parents yet because I didn't want to freak out my mom. She's been on edge lately and I didn't want to add to it."

"That's probably a good idea, but you will have to tell her sooner or later. Do you want me to call your dad?"

Harper cringed but agreed that Tab should probably tell him. That way he could handle her mom. "You can call him, but please tell him not to tell mom until I'm on the way there."

"Will do. Meantime, I'm going to get you an escort out of town. We don't know who this guy was or what he wanted. I'll feel better once you get here."

"Me too, and thanks for everything. I'm going to run inside and grab my stuff and get on the way. I kind of hate to leave my house with no one home. He may try to come back."

"Harper, that is not for you to worry about. I will have an officer there around the clock, and when we get back, I'll look into this myself. Be careful and call when you're on the way." Tab hung up and dialed Griff's phone hating to lay this latest chain of events on him. He would go crazy if anything were to happen to Harper or any of his family. It rang and rang and went to voicemail. He felt a little relieved and decided not to leave a message. Griff would see that he called and call him back soon enough. And Harper was out of danger, so he didn't feel an urgency to add to his best friend's stress right away. He'll know soon enough.

#

Abby and Griff were having dinner at Ruth's Chris Steakhouse inside the Hard Rock Casino. It was one of Abby's favorite places, and he wanted her to enjoy herself. She finally slept a little when they got there and was feeling good.

Earlier, Griff returned to the hotel around 5:30pm and joined Abby in the Casino. They didn't usually go to dinner late, but he could only get reservations for 7:30pm. Olivia and Jack arrived around 5:30, and they were going to join Abby and Griff after they checked into their hotel room. He figured they would be up later than usual, so the time didn't matter. Abby was delighted to be there. She had always been a steak and potato kind of girl. Griff used to love it too, but now they were both trying to limit the red meat they ate. They arrived around 7:15pm and were seated right away. They waited for Olivia and Jack to get there. He told her about his afternoon with the guys and the unfortunate news that they did not see the Dodge Dart.

Griff told her how they spent the afternoon tailgating and watching all the old cars that came into town. They took turns walking into the coliseum and looking around. With three of them, they were able to spread out a little and still keep watch. And now that Jack had arrived, they could cover more territory when they set out the following day.

Abby offered to come and help, but he shot the idea down right away. He didn't want her anywhere around if they find this guy. They don't know enough about his motives yet, but they do know he's an ex-cop. And they at least now know what he looks like. Griff figured if this guy doesn't want to be found, they won't find him. The only good thing going for them was that they didn't think he knew they were on to him yet. They left everything at the house just as they found it. The element of surprise was what they were hoping for. It was probably their only hope.

When Griff left Tab and Trey earlier that afternoon, they were still looking around and were headed to get something to eat. He extended an invitation to them both to join them for dinner at Ruth's, but Tab thought it would be better that they split up. It was already going to be like finding a needle in a haystack, so the more ground they could cover the better. Tab knew that it was a good possibility that the guy would be in Biloxi and never cross paths with them. They hoped that wouldn't be the case.

It was now 7:30pm and Jack and Olivia joined them. It was good to see his wife light up when her best friend came in. Still no word from Harper, but she should be there soon. He was definitely more relaxed, but until his daughter was there safe, he wouldn't be happy. He did speak to Alex earlier and they were in Baton Rouge for the weekend. Gabby had a gymnastics competition, so they decided to make a weekend of it. E.R. was with them, and Griff was grateful for that. All of his family should be safe this weekend. So why did he feel like something was wrong? Around 8:15pm he got the strangest feeling come over him that he hadn't been able to shake. He chalked it up to everything going on and tried to forget about it.

Griff brought Jack up to speed, and they talked about their plans for the next day. Jack did not like to gamble, so he was pleased to know that they would be out at *Crusin' the Coast* instead of in the casino. When he got home earlier today, his wife informed him that they had to go to Biloxi with Abby and Griff. Of course, he agreed, but Biloxi was not one of his favorite places to visit. He considered Griff a good friend and was glad to be there to help him.

Griff excused himself to go to the restroom. On his way, his phone rang, and it was Tab. He had been waiting to hear from him, so he answered quickly. He barely got to say hello when Tab began to fill him in on what happened at home earlier with Harper.

A hundred unanswered questions were running through Griff's mind as Tab told him detail by detail what happened. Tab, being in the profession he was in, was very thorough, and when he was finished Griff was speechless.

His first thought was, *What the hell was Harper doing at the house? She was not supposed to go anywhere around there.* His second thought was *Abby's going to kill her!* And the questions kept coming. *Was the intruder Detective Hawkins, the man we are looking for or just a weird coincidence? Are we wasting our time here if he is there? What would he be looking for at the house? How do I tell Abby any of this?*

Now, he had to decide when to tell Abby. Should he wait until tomorrow because she was having such a good time? Harper was on her way there and no longer in danger. There was no good reason to tell her tonight. He thought he might not tell her until they were heading home. Griff knew his wife would be mad that he kept this from her but hoped she would get over it, she always did.

His youngest daughter was going to be the death of them yet. She had always been fearless to the point of it becoming dangerous. She thought she was invincible. She had always been headstrong and very stubborn. The last few years had been more difficult, because she was now an adult and thought she knew everything. She was naive to danger and that scared Griff.

He dialed Harpers number and braced himself for yet another battle. But this one he intended on winning. She messed up and he was going to make sure she realized it.

CHAPTER 22

Harper hated when her father treated her like a baby. He was acting like this was her fault. She was glad he was not going to tell her mother until later. It had been one heck of a day, and she didn't feel like dealing with more drama.

With everything going on, she didn't have a chance to text Noah. He sent her a text earlier, but she didn't see it. She was hoping to get together with him when they arrived that night, but now it was so late. She thought she'd just text him back and let him know she was in Biloxi and hoped to see him over the weekend.

They didn't arrive at the *Golden Nugget* until 11:00pm and after unloading the car it was 11:30pm. Harper sent Noah a text, apologized for it being so late and told him that she was in Biloxi with her parents. To her delight, he responded right away and seemed happy that she was there. Now she had to decide if she and Henly were going out or going to bed. She was not tired at all and really would like to see Noah.

She and Henly discussed their plans and decided to go downstairs by the bar. She sent Noah another text and told him where they were going to be. Harper and Henly were both only 20 years old but had very impressive fake ID's.

After showering and dressing they met up with her parents and their friends for a while. Her mom looked like she was having fun. Her parents had always liked music and dancing. Her father's favorite music was rock and roll, especially, songs from the Rolling Stones. He had attended every concert they've had within driving distance. The band tonight played a lot of that type of music. Harper was grateful that the music was loud, because she made the mistake of telling her mother that Noah would be meeting her there later. They hung out with Harper and Henly for a while but decided to head up to bed around 1:30am. Her dad had a lot to do the next day and needed to get some sleep.

Harper walked to the bar for a drink while looking at her cell phone to see if she had a text from Noah. Not paying attention, she ran right into someone and knocked them backwards to the ground. She looked up and realized it was Noah. She quickly looked around for her parents but was relieved to see that they were already gone. She wasn't trying to hide him from them, but her mother could be overwhelming sometimes. She would like to get to know him a little before she introduced him to them.

Noah smiled, "I was hoping to run into you but not literally."

Harper tried not to laugh but couldn't help it. She extended her hand to help him up and apologized.

"If it makes you feel any better, I was reading your text." He didn't seem mad, so that was a point in his favor. You had to have a sense of humor if you wanted to hang with her. She was like her mother that way. They both laughed at everything even if they shouldn't.

"Surprisingly, it does. Where are your parents and Henly?"

"My parents went up to bed like two seconds ago. You just missed them, thank goodness. Not because of you, because of them. You met my mother at the restaurant already, and since then she's been obsessed with you. She's weird that way. My dad is pretty cool under normal circumstances, but he's on edge lately. We have a lot of stuff going on." Harper trailed off thinking of the phone conversation with her dad earlier. He was really upset with her. You would think he would be a little bit happy, because if she hadn't gone home, they may not have known that someone entered the house. She knew it could have gotten bad, but it didn't.

"I thought your mom was nice when I met her. What does your dad do?"

"He's supposed to be retiring but he still goes to the office almost every day."

She noticed Henly talking to a guy across the room. That was so odd for her, she was normally so shy.

"You said you were here for work, what do you do?"

"Right now, I'm working at the D. A's office. I just graduated from Loyola and trying to decide if I want to go to law school or not. That's my father's dream for me and at one time it was mine too. Lately, I'm not so sure. I think I would rather be out there making a difference for people. I really like detective work, so I thought I'd spend some time doing that before deciding. Of course, my father is not too happy about it, but he's trying to let me make my own way. In fact, it was he who got me the job. My boss is an old friend of his from college. He agreed to let me tag along for a few months and that's what I'm doing. I have to say though; I really like it so far. It helps that the guys I'm working with are so good at their jobs." Noah, realizing he was rambling on asked, "So what about you? What's your story?"

"I'm an Esthetician. I do make-up for a living. I never did like school, and I love doing someone's makeup and watching their transformation. Don't get me wrong, sometimes I keep it simple and just bring out their natural beauty. It all depends on the client and what they want. I also do spray tanning. I thought my parents were going to flip when I said I didn't want to go to college, but instead wanted to do makeup. Surprisingly, they agreed and here I am. My dad does not understand why people would spend that kind of money to get their makeup done. He calls it 'war paint' for the 'painted ponies.' He's very 'old school" if you know what I mean. I attended a six-month program that covered everything I need to know about skin types and stuff like that. The actual makeup part I learned from hours and hours of watching YouTube videos. I used to use my cousin as a model, and she used me. We are both rather good but I'm the only one who chose it as a career choice."

"So, you work for yourself?"

"Yes, actually I do. My mom turned our pool house into a little makeup studio for me. It needed to be fixed because since Hurricane Katrina the roof leaked, and we hadn't been able to find someone who could fix it. We had several people come out and try but it never lasted. And each time we had someone change out the sheetrock and paint it. Finally, mom found someone a few months ago who fixed it the right way and it hasn't leaked since. And this time she decided to do the sheetrock work herself. We painted everything together and decided to make it into my studio. I get pretty booked up on most weekends but I'm still building my client list." Harper looked around the room for Henly. She and the guy she was talking to were dancing on the far edge of the dance floor.

"Do you know that guy Henly is dancing with? I don't recognize him and it's so unlike her to be dancing with someone she doesn't know."

Noah having met Henly with Harper the first time they met, glanced in the direction she was looking and spotted her. The guy she was dancing with happened to be someone he went to Loyola with. They never hung out or anything, but they had a few classes together. That's one of the reasons he thought he'd be good at investigating because he was very observant.

"I don't know him personally, but I do remember him from some of my classes at Loyola," Noah shared, with a surprised tone of voice.

"Well maybe we should go over there and introduce ourselves," Harper announced as she grabbed his hand and lead him across the floor. As children, she had always looked out for Henly, and it was no different now. Her best friend was the sweetest person in the world, but she could be very naïve when it came to boys.

She sized up the guy before they reached them and had to admit, he was rather good looking. He looked to be about six foot tall, had dark hair and it was clear that he worked out. By the way, her friend was looking at him, she must have thought the same thing.

"Hey Henly, introduce us to your friend." Harper extended her hand to shake his. They made the introductions and acknowledged that he and Noah were in some classes together. His name was Oliver Arseneau, and he was from France. He had been attending Loyola for the past four years and loved New Orleans. Henly obviously liked him, and he seemed nice enough. They spent the next few hours dancing and laughing and enjoying the evening. Harper was feeling so happy, compared to how things were going earlier that night at her house. She was so rattled by everything and hated leaving her home unattended. By the time they drove to Biloxi, she was more relaxed and relieved to be away from there. Never in a million years did Harper think she would be having this much fun just a few hours later.

They all decided to go for something to eat, but first, she and Henly went to the restroom. They were laughing and talking about both of their new guys. Again, she was not paying attention, but this time someone bumped into her. It was so crowded and loud in there, but she was quite sure she heard him whisper something. By the time she looked back, he was gone, and it was too crowded to even try to follow him. Did she really hear something or just imagined it? She stopped walking and looked at Henly. She told her what just happened, and her friend assured her that she was just being paranoid again. After a few moments, she shook it off and agreed, and they hurried to the restroom. She was not going to let anyone, or anything ruin the night, or rather, morning. It was almost 4am, but she was really enjoying Noah's company and didn't want the night to end. She tucked what just happened away for now, but she will definitely be paying more attention to her surroundings. If someone was following her, she would find out. It might just take some smart planning first. Her parents thought she was naïve, but she wasn't, and she could take care of herself. In fact, this might just be a reason for Noah to stay around and help her, with him wanting to be an investigator and all. She knew exactly what to do next: fill them in.

#

Abby and Griff were back in their room and ready for bed. Griff noticed his wife had her usual glow about her that he was so familiar with. Lately, she had been acting odd, but tonight she seemed to be her old self again. He really hated the idea that he had to destroy her good mood sooner or later. He can't keep the break in from her forever. He just hoped she could rejuvenate enough to be able to handle it. The fact that Harper was at the house when it happened could put her over the edge. She still saw her as her baby girl, not a grown woman.

He felt the same way, but he knew his daughter was a tough one. He had been impressed at how she was handling all of this. When he called Harper earlier, after Tab told him what happened, she was calmer than he thought she would be. He tried to make her see how dangerous the situation was that she was in but ended up yelling at her. She was right when she came back with the point that they would not have even known someone was in the house unless she had gone there, but agreed, that knowledge was not worth her life.

A few years back, Harper took some self-defense classes with Abby and Alex. At first, she was not too happy about it, but then she really enjoyed the classes and caught on quickly. He had to say his daughter may look dainty, but given the chance, she could hurt someone. That made him feel a little better, but none of that mattered if that same someone had a gun. That's what he can't seem to get Harper to realize. He knew she was probably her own worst enemy.

Abby had been watching her husband all night long and knew he was keeping something from her. They had a great time at dinner with Olivia and Jack and afterwards danced the night away. She couldn't quite put her finger on it, but something was going on with him. They both were under a lot of stress lately, but he was acting strange in a different way. She started noticing him behaving differently after dinner, but she didn't know what had changed. He said he spoke to Tab, so it had to be something to do with that phone call. She thought maybe he was worried about Harper driving there because she always drove dangerously fast. But she had arrived a while ago and he was still acting peculiar. If it hadn't been so late, she would have confronted him, but it had been such a nice day that she just wanted peace for a few more hours. But she went to bed determined to get to the bottom of things the next day and find out exactly what he was hiding.

CHAPTER 23

SEPTEMBER 1997

The news reporters stood outside the site of the gruesome murder waiting for what little information they could get on this high-profile case. All they knew at that point was that the site belonged to a well-known football player and that there was a body found outside by the pool. The crime scene had been blocked off and the police were investigating.

Word on the street was that the property was newly acquired by the Dallas Cowboys second string quarterback Morton McCalister. It was purchased just weeks before in a small town called Osyka in Mississippi. There was no word on if he was at the property at the time or of his involvement.

#

He walked through the halls of what he would call a mansion; tucked away, out in the middle of nowhere. When he received the call about a murder in Osyka, he was taken by surprise. Osyka was a small town and was usually quiet. Sure, they had the usual, like traffic violations, disturbing the peace violations and even drug violations, but never murder. Detective Hawkins couldn't remember ever investigating a murder in those parts.

As he walked through the house, he took notice of all the blood on the floor, down the hallway, and towards the back of the house. The call reported one body, but there was a lot of blood for only one person. As he approached the kitchen, he could see officers out towards the pool taping off an area. Instead of going out to investigate, he decided to do a walk-through of the house.

It appeared the conflict originated in the house and ended out by the pool. He noticed blood on the railing of the stairs leading to or maybe from the second floor. It appeared to be someone's handprints. He followed the trail, and that lead him to another staircase, leading to a third floor. That was odd, because from outside, it appeared to be only two stories, but old houses like this often had many stories.

Detective Hawkins proceeded with caution, because apparently, he was the first to check out the house. When the call came in, he was on I-55 right by the Osyka exit. It only took him 5 minutes to arrive on the scene. He notified the local police of his presence and began his own investigation. He had always had a good relationship with the law enforcement in all the small towns in the area. That had proven to be extremely helpful to him.

The trails of blood led him to the hallway, to the right of the stairs on the second floor. That's where he noticed a gruesome scene of blood splattered all over the place.

He was immediately reminded of the cases that haunted him at night. They too, were horrific scenes of brutal beatings, where the bodies were not only unidentifiable, but some were unrecognizable as a human.

There were doors on all sides of the hallway, but most of the blood was by the smallest one. It looked like some sort of chute for clothes that would transfer the clothes from the second floor to the first, most likely to a laundry room. There was blood splattered on the door and the surrounding walls, which indicated some kind of struggle took place there. There was a table next to the door that had been knocked over, and the vase that once sat on top, now lay broken on the floor.

The odd thing was that there were no other trails of blood, except the handprints along the stairs. Certainly, this much blood should be accompanied with a body to go with it. At the very least, there should be a trail of blood that led to a body elsewhere. Maybe they used the chute for an escape or were pushed into it. There's only one way to find out.

"Detective Hawkins are you up there?" a voice coming from the stairs startled him.

"Yes, I am. I was getting ready to open this door to see why there is so much blood around it. There's no apparent trail that would explain what happened to the person this blood came from. If it is from our victim outside, how did he get there without a trail from up here?"

The officer reached the top of the stairs and stood next to Detective Hawkins. He inspected the area and determined that Detective Hawkins was right. The answer to where all the blood was coming from was behind that door.

Detective Hawkins carefully opened the door and they both looked in. As suspected, there was a body at the bottom of the chute, lying still on top of a pile of clothes. Again, Detective Hawkins thought that there was a lot of blood, but it appeared the body wasn't as damaged as the others from his previous cases. It was not beaten beyond recognition, thankfully.

Maybe the victim was able to get away from the attacker by getting into the chute. As they were assessing the scene, Detective Hawkins noticed movement from the body at the bottom of the chute. He yelled, to the officer that the victim was still alive, and ran down the stairs in the direction he thought the laundry room would be, with the officer in tow. He instructed the officer to get the paramedics from outside, while he raced to find the laundry room.

Within seconds, the paramedics were there assessing the female victim in the laundry chute. After some time, they got the victim stabilized and were administering oxygen. She was still breathing, but barely. They carefully excavated the body from where it was trapped. She had a large gash on her forehead, probably where most of the blood came from. As much as he wished she would stay until she regained consciousness and he could get a statement from her, he knew they needed to get to the hospital quickly. Knowing he needed to make sure to cover every inch of the scene, just in case, he decided to continue where he left off when he found that female victim, and headed back upstairs.

After the upstairs was all clear, he headed back down to check the rest of the house. He noticed a lot of exercise clothes in one of the bedrooms. That seemed to be the only common link between all of his cases. The people committing the crimes were all into some sort of exercise. He knew it was farfetched, but he was certain that was the link that would bring the answers to all his questions.

He went room to room and at last he found a workout room full of equipment. There slouched down, hidden in the corner, was a person with a face full of blood, who was babbling. Detective Hawkins was positive he knew exactly what he was babbling, "Look Within and Be Careful". It was just like all the others. He quickly assessed the situation and the suspect and motioned to the officer in the other room to come in. He whispered to the officer to get the paramedics again, being careful not to provoke the suspect who appeared to be incoherent. Before the others got there, he made a quick sweep of the room and determined the suspect did not appear to be armed with any weapon. There was, however, a tall walking stick on the floor a few feet away and it was full of blood, which meant it was probably the murder weapon.

CHAPTER 24

2017

After having breakfast with their wives, Griff and Jack left to meet up with Tab and Trey. They wanted to get an early start and hopefully cross paths with the man they were all looking for. This was the busiest day of the entire *Crusin' the Coast* week, and if you didn't get out early, you would be in bumper-to-bumper traffic all day. The plan was to get close to the Coliseum again and observe the cars going by.

Griff knew it was a long shot, but it was the only thing they can do. It was clear when they went to Summit, that the detective had not been there in a long time. Attempts to locate him have come up empty. If he was the man that was in their house last night, he knew they were not home. Tab said the intruder knew where the key was and the alarm code, so, obviously he had done his homework. Griff was also confident that Detective Hawkins knew exactly where Abby was, and that scared the heck out of him.

Tab and Trey were already parked by the Coliseum. Griff found a place a few blocks down, parked, and walked back to them. They talked over the plan and decided to split up into twos, so they could cover more area. It was agreed that Griff and Tab would go into the coliseum first to look around and then meet back at the truck in an hour. Trey and Jack were going to watch out for the car. They all agreed to start asking around to see if anyone saw the Dodge Dart in the area. Thank God they were looking for a unique car.

"Man, there are a lot of people in here. It'll be a miracle if we actually find this guy. Can I see that photo of him again?" Tab wanted to make sure it was fresh in his mind.

Griff pulled out the picture of Detective Clay Hawkins and handed it to Tab. "And you know as well as I do, it's only going to get worse as the day goes on. I think over the last few years, *Cruisin' the Coast* has become one of the biggest car auctions in the area. It helps that it's held in the Fall because the weather tends to bring people out."

They grabbed something to drink and found a centrally located place to sit and watch.

"Did you tell Abby about what happened last night? I've been worried all night about that. I didn't want to ask you in front of Jack in case you hadn't told anyone yet. I talked to the officer who watched the house last night and he said everything was quiet. I do suspect it was Detective Hawkins but can't for the life of me figure out what he wants with Abby or why he broke into your house. What could possibly be the connection? He must have been looking for something, but what?" Tab looked concerned as he waited for Griff's response.

"No, I didn't tell Abby or anyone yet. This is the first time in weeks she's actually relaxing, so I didn't want to upset her. I think I'm going to tell her on the way home."

"I completely understand man. That's probably a good idea"

"I've been going over and over all the things we do know so far, and really can't come up with a connection either. The fact that the detective is from the Brookhaven area, leads me to believe we had to cross paths with him when we were at the camp in Magnolia. We don't go towards Summit too often, but on our last trip we spent a few hours there. Abby was looking for an old antique walking stick, so we went to the shops there and then had lunch. We weren't there that long, maybe a few hours, and I don't recall talking to anyone. We definitely did not talk to or even see Detective Hawkins. There were a few ladies in the shops we went into and only a hand full of people at the restaurant." Griff's voice was heavy, and he looked worn out.

"Did Abby find a walking stick?"

"Yes, she did at the last shop we went into. A lot of the shops had new ones, but that was not what she was looking for. In fact, we were walking out the store when this old lady approached her holding an old walking stick, exactly the kind Abby wanted. Now that I'm thinking about it, something about the old lady seemed odd to me and made me extremely uncomfortable. The feeling passed so quickly that I forgot about it, until now. Tab, I tell you, it was as if the dead passed through me. I think I even shivered. It sounds kind of crazy, and just in time for Halloween." With that, both men laughed an uneasy kind of laugh, and then sat in silence for a while.

Tab broke the silence and went on to say, "I guess, depending on what happens here today, we should head to that shop in Summit and see if there's a connection between the store, the old lady, and Detective Hawkins. You never know in small towns who people are related to. I don't suppose you caught her name?"

"No, as I mentioned before, we were on our way out and after the feeling I got when I saw her, I walked out the store to get the car. I can't even recall what she looked like. Abby walked to the register to pay and then met me by the car. We were talking and laughing the whole way back, and like I said, I never thought about it again. And from what I could tell, Abby didn't have the same reaction I did. She was excited that we were able to find a stick and seemed happy and content all the way back home."

They continued to watch the crowd and began to get a little discouraged. Now, Griff couldn't stop thinking about that old woman. *Was she the connection?* From what he could remember, she was old and fragile looking. Abby was only with her for a few minutes, and as far as he could remember, they didn't even talk to each other.

Still lost in his thoughts, Griff almost toppled over when Tab shoved him.

Tab laughed and said, "Earth to Griff! What planet were you on man? I think it's about time we go meet the guys back by the car and get some lunch."

Just as they were walking up to the truck, Tab's phone rang. It was Trey.

Sounding anxious on the other end of the phone Trey shouted, "We got eyes on the car! It's heading our way, and I think the traffic is slow enough that we might have a chance to surround him. Where are y'all?"

Trey turned just as Griff and Tab came around the truck to join him and Jack. He hung up the phone, helped Tab and Griff into the back of the truck, and handed Tab the binoculars. The car was still a few blocks down and at a red light.

As far as Tab could tell, Trey was right; it was a Blue Dodge Dart. They couldn't make out who was driving yet. Trey informed them that Jack took off on foot towards the car to see if he could confirm it was the detective and give them some time to react. They didn't want to spook him or give him a chance to get away. There were a few streets he could turn up if he wanted to get away and they wouldn't be able to catch him.

Griff suddenly became nervous. This was so important, not only to his wife's safety, but after last night, his whole family's safety. He listened to Tab lay out a plan and tried to stay focused. The car was in the left lane traveling east, but there were so many people.

Jack called to report that the windows were tinted, so it was impossible to make a positive identification on the driver. He was going to stay behind the car walking in case the driver realized something was up and tried to run. He sent the license plate number to Tab who confirmed that the car was registered to Detective Hawkins. They needed to quickly decide what to do next. Not being able to positively identify the driver changed the plan. Who knew what he would do if they tried to apprehend him or if he was armed? He hadn't displayed any aggression yet and until they know what he wanted; they don't want to put anyone in danger unnecessarily.

Tab pointed out, "We have to assume this guy knows what you look like Griff. He was at the top of his game as a detective, and that doesn't just go away. If he did his homework, and I'm sure he did, he would have all kinds of information on your family. The good thing is he hasn't shown violence in any way yet. I think you need to stay far enough away, so that he's not tipped off that we're on to him." Tab continued, "Trey, you cross the street and try to keep eyes on him at all times. Try not to let the car get too far ahead of you. It looks like traffic is at a crawl right up to the next light, but after that it's moving a little faster. We really need to approach him before the next light. Griff, maybe you should get up in front of him. Just pull that cap down a little and stay in the crowds."

Griff, now on the verge of panic, nodded in agreement. He couldn't remember ever being this scared in his life. But his family had never been threatened like this before.

If it were a situation that had only been affecting him, he would be nervous of course, but not to this degree. He said a quick prayer and drew from his faith to calm himself down and meet the task in front of him head on.

"I'm ready. Let's do this." Griff set off to get in position.

The other two men got in position. The light changed to green a few minutes ago, but thankfully, traffic had slowed down to stop and go. This was good for them, but the anticipation was killing Griff, and Tab hoped he could contain himself. Tab understood where Griff was coming from because he knew if this were his family, he would also have a hard time keeping control.

Tab walked toward the car slowly. He allowed it to pass him, so that he could try to see in the windshield. Just as Jack said, it was too dark to see anything. The one thing that stood out to Tab was that most of the vehicles at the event had their windows down, so why would he keep his up, other than to avoid being seen.

It suddenly began to drizzle. Griff laughed to himself at the irony, *Of course, you can't have a car chase without rain.* He quickly realized what was not funny was that the crowds were running for cover. Thankfully, some people stayed and endured the rain, so he was able to continue his plan, and get close to the car as it inched near him. He had been watching the car approach from the distance and feeling his heart rate rise with every inch it gained. He had eyes on both Tab and Trey. Griff wondered how close Tab was going to let him get to the light before doing something. Keeping his eyes glued to Tab and the car, Griff noticed Tab walking up to the driver's side. With the traffic moving like it was, he was able to tap on the window. There was no response, so he taped again. The car continued to roll forward at a crawl, but whoever was driving was ignoring Tab. Griff walked toward the car slowly. No way was he going to let him get past that light without at least knowing who was behind the wheel.

Tab reached in his pocket and pulled out his badge. He tapped one more time and held the badge up to the window. At that moment, the door sprung open and knocked Tab back into the crowd. The man from inside the car took off running back towards the coliseum. Griff's reaction was to take off running after him, along with Jack, Tab, and Trey.

Tab was furious with himself for not seeing that coming. The suspect only had a short lead on them, but because Tab was able to regain balance quickly, he was sure he could catch him. The crowd certainly didn't help, but he did notice Griff gaining on the man and Tab dug in harder. He was not sure what Griff would do and would rather be the one to catch him. Not to mention, they still didn't know if he was armed.

All four of the men were still pursuing the suspect, but Griff was still the closest. The suspect ran down a side street leading to the back of the coliseum, and to their benefit it was a lot less crowded. The bad thing was that there was a main street back there, with several more side streets. If he reached them, their chances were going to be slim to keep up with him.

Griff had been hot on the heels of this guy since he bolted out of the car. There was no way he was letting him get away. He still couldn't make out whether or not it was the detective, but whoever it was knew something was up and didn't want to be caught. He was so close he could feel the wind coming from the man in front of him who was in full gate. Times like this was when Griff was happy that he attended spinning class three times a week.

His mind was racing, his heart was pounding, and he knew now was the time to make a move. With that thought, he leapt forward and took down the man running from him. He landed on top of him, and they began to struggle. Tab and Trey were right behind Griff, and the three of them gained control of the man. Jack, who was the furthest away, came up behind them. Finally, all four men surrounded the suspect, relieved to have him detained. Now it was time for some answers.

CHAPTER 25

After they got the day started, Abby and Olivia decided to do some shopping before lunch. They wanted to go over to the *Beau Rivage Casino* because they had several shops inside the hotel, and it was away from the traffic. She couldn't remember the last time she was this relaxed. She still had her guard up but, felt like there was safety in numbers. Griff wanted her to stay in the room, but he knew that was not going to happen. She did promise him to stay with Olivia, and that was exactly what she was going to do. She wanted Harper to join them, but when she called her earlier for breakfast, she was not ready to get up. They had a late-night last night, which meant she would probably sleep half the day.

She didn't get a chance to talk to Harper about Noah and was dying to know the details. She wanted her to be happy and to move on with her life. The young man seemed like a nice guy and more importantly, from what Harper told her about their first encounter, he knew how to handle her. She could be a firecracker and as stubborn as they come. A lot of boys were scared off because of her strong independence, but Abby had a feeling Noah was up for the task. It was going to kill her to wait for the details, but hopefully she and Olivia would stay busy until her daughter graced them with her presence. No doubt, Harper would be calling the minute she woke up, ready to eat.

Abby and Olivia decided to take a shuttle to the *Beau Rivage*. There was way too much traffic to drive and while it was within walking distance, it would be a long walk with packages, and there would absolutely be packages. She didn't break the bank, but she did win a little last night. She planned on spending that money on something instead of putting it right back into the casino.

As they stood outside waiting for the shuttle, Abby noticed just how many people were there, which meant they had a long time to wait. Luckily, the air was cool and crisp, and they decided to just enjoy the day. When the shuttle finally arrived, the crowd started moving forward. A man bumped into her and then passed her up. She got that feeling in the back of her neck she gets when something isn't right, but she couldn't get a look at him. He boarded the shuttle and within seconds, the bus was full. She watched the shuttle leave and could swear he was watching her the whole time. His face was shadowed but she could tell that he was tall and wearing a baseball cap. Olivia smacked her and brought her out of her thoughts. The shuttle was gone, and she was left feeling a little silly. She was sure it was just a coincidence and probably someone who was anxious and impatient to get to the car show. There was no shortage of those types of people out.

She suggested to Olivia that they walk to the *Beau Rivage*, since it would be about fifteen minutes until the next shuttle arrived. Olivia agreed and the two of them set off on their walk. For a moment, she felt guilty knowing that Griff would not want her out on the street. But soon, the conversation with Olivia had her laughing and forgetting everything except the feeling of being watched, a feeling she'd had since they left the *Golden Nugget.* The guy who bumped into her on his way into the shuttle didn't help things.

Her anxiety level went up a little as they approached the *Beau Rivage*. She could see a shuttle bus there, but it looked empty. Now she wished she would've watched to see if the shuttle came there first or went in a different direction. Sometimes they go to several casinos for pickups. They didn't check the route before they left, but she thought it was going to go straight there. She looked around to see if there was anyone suspicious looking. She almost laughed out loud at that thought because there were a lot of suspicious people there. It didn't appear that anyone was watching her now, so she began to relax.

It was just as crowded inside the *Beau Rivage* as it was outside. Abby decided she wanted to look for some Christmas presents while she was there. Most of the stores stocked Vera Bradley, and both Harper and Alex loved her line. This year, she thought she might get Alex a leather purse from Fossil. She gave her one years ago and she still used it. The women spent another hour or so shopping and several times during that time, Abby got the feeling she was being watched. She knew she was probably being paranoid but couldn't seem to stop the feelings from gripping her with fear. Taking a deep breath, she announced she was ready for lunch. What she was really ready for was a glass of wine or maybe two. She needed something to take the edge off before she lost it.

She was also worried about Griff and the guys. He usually checked in by now, but she knew things were chaotic out there. She hoped they could find this guy and get to the bottom of things soon, but at the same time, she knew it could be dangerous. Lord how she missed their boring, everyday lives.

They walked towards the back of the casino to a little café. She told Olivia to go get a table while she went to the restroom. There was a long hallway leading to the women's bathroom. For a second, Abby hesitated but again brushed the feeling off and headed down the hall. As she came out of the door from the ladies' room, a hand came over her mouth and another around her waist and she found herself being pulled backwards. Her first thought was, *Griff's going to kill me*, and her next thought was, *Fight!*

Olivia was starting to worry about Abby. It had only been about five minutes, but she should have been back by now. She probably should have gone with Abby to the bathroom, after all, they did promise Griff to stay together. She headed to the bathroom with a sense of urgency and prayed her friend was alright.

#

The last few minutes seemed to last forever. From the time Griff noticed the suspect bolting from the car until now, everything appeared to be moving in slow motion. Luckily, Tab had handcuffs with him, and they secured the suspect and made sure he was clean of weapons. Everyone was catching their breath and regrouping. It seemed like no one wanted to state the obvious, it was not the detective.

Tab found an area that was secluded, so they could question the suspect without an audience. He knew Griff was disappointed by the look on his face, but at least they knew it was the detective's car, and maybe this guy knew something of his whereabouts.

Tab sized up the suspect and was afraid he was not going to be much help. He looked like a kid, maybe 17 or 18 and his clothes suggested he may even be living on the streets. He did have a wallet that held a single 20-dollar bill in it and nothing else. He was extremely thin and frail, and his rotten teeth suggested prolonged drug use.

Griff started the questioning. "Where is the owner of that car? What's your name?"

"Whoa, back up man." Tab grabbed Griff and pulled him off the suspect and whispered to him to please let him handle this. "Let's give the man some space."

Trey added, "It looks like you might need to sit down a minute. Maybe you can sit on these crates here."

"Can you tell me who owns that car?"

The suspect just sat there with a terrified look on his face. Clearly, he was coming down from a high and was nervous as hell. Tab knew he could probably get him to talk, but his gut was telling him he didn't have anything to tell.

"Look, we need to locate the guy who owns that car. Do you know him?"

The suspect shook his head, no.

Again, Tab asked, "Do you know the owner of that car?"

With a shaky voice, the suspect replied, "Hey man, I don't want any trouble. Some guy gave me fifty bucks to drive his car. He said he had another car he needed to bring to the show and couldn't drive both. I didn't steal the car if that's what you're thinking. I just was supposed to keep the car moving up and down Hwy 90 with the rest of the old cars. I knew something was strange about that guy because who would just let a stranger drive a nice car like that."

"Where did you pick up the car?"

"I didn't pick it up. The man approached me down in the Edgewood Mall parking lot. I was just minding my own business you know, and he approached me. I never saw that guy before in my life. And he offered me fifty bucks. You can have the car, just let me go okay."

Tab stared at the suspect for a few minutes. He pulled Griff to the side and said, "I was afraid of this, I don't think he knows anything. Detective Hawkins is smart and is not about to let a drug addict know anything that could help us."

"Can you describe the man who offered you the fifty dollars?"

"Like I said, I never saw him before. He was a tall thin older man. He's wearing a baseball cap. That's all I remember."

This can't be happening. Griff was so sure they were going to get some answers this weekend. Now what were they supposed to do. Tab was right. This guy didn't know much. He was probably a decoy, but why? This set Griff off wondering if the detective was still in Biloxi or was he long gone. He had a sudden urge to call Abby and check in. When he stepped away to dial, Abby's phone went to voicemail. Of course, he was immediately worried and wondered where she could be? She knew how tense things were, and he knew she would definitely have the phone close just in case. Frustrated, he hung up and made a mental note to call again in a few minutes. He hoped she would call back between then.

Tab suggested they ask a few more questions then let the guy go. They decided that Trey and Jack would tail him to see if he met up with Detective Hawkins. They also told the guy he could go back to the car and drive it to wherever he was supposed to take it.

"It's real important that we talk to the owner of that car. By the way, where were you supposed to deliver it?"

The man looked to be feeling a little better. He stood up and straightened his clothes as best he could. He looked up at Tab and said, "I was supposed to drop it off at the *Golden Nugget* this afternoon."

Griff's world began to spin. He stood paralyzed with terror. Abby was at the *Golden Nugget*. She was not alone because she promised Griff that she would stay with Olivia, and the *Golden Nugget* was packed with people, inside and out. It was already packed when he left that morning. Was that the plan? Distract them while he got to Abby. If he had all that information about the house, including the alarm code, chances were, he knew what room they were in at the *Golden Nugget*. When he left her this morning, they were already downstairs having breakfast. She and Olivia were discussing what they were going to do all day. He did recall them talking about going to the spa. Maybe that's why she didn't answer the phone earlier. She needed to call him now.

He could feel his heartbeat in his ears ready to explode. All he could think of was to run. At that, he found himself taking off at a sprint, towards the street in front of the Coliseum. While running, he took out his phone and dialed her number again, but still no answer. He knew he couldn't possibly run the whole way because it was probably about six or seven miles. He was, however, going to run until the traffic was moving steady and then get a ride the rest of the way.

He turned to look back and Tab was right on his heels. He heard him yell that Jack took off on the back streets to try and get a ride that way. Trey stayed with the suspect. Together now, they were running at a speed that physical limitations would soon shut down. *How did I not see this coming?* The street below his feet and the crowds all around Griff blurred as he felt a surge of adrenaline. He'd run the whole way if he had to. All he could focus on was the love of his life, Abby, and how he had let her down. He just hoped he was not too late.

CHAPTER 26

It was about 12:30pm, and Harper and Henly were up and ready for some lunch. Her mother called early in the morning and left her a message inviting them to breakfast, but they had a late night and needed to get some sleep. She could really sleep all day but was hoping to spend some time with Noah again today.

She called her mother about thirty minutes ago, and it went to voicemail. Harper was not normally paranoid but for some reason, today she was feeling anxious. She blamed it on the break-in at her house the night before. She had to admit, she was really scared. More so after watching the video and realizing the man knew a lot about her family. And last night, she was sure that a man whispered something to her. She planned on telling both her father and Tab about it today. She didn't want to tell her mother and upset her but felt her father should know.

She brushed it all off, and they both finished getting ready for the day. She wanted to spend a little extra time getting ready in case she happened to meet up with Noah. He said he would be working all day and would check in with her when he could. He didn't say what he was actually doing, but he must get a lunch break. Before they left to meet her mother, she was going to text him just in case he was free for lunch.

Henly had been quiet all morning. The night before really did a number on her too. She didn't even like scary movies, and she only went into haunted houses when Harper made her. She did look happy late last night when she met Oliver. *Maybe she's thinking about Oliver,* Harper guessed.

"Henly, did you hear from Oliver yet today?"

With a dreamy look on her face she replied, "Not yet, but he did say he would call me after 5pm. We did stay out pretty late last night, and maybe he already had plans today. He's probably going to the car show at the Coliseum; I think that's why he's here in Biloxi."

"How are you feeling aside from the new love in your life? I know things got really tense at my house, and things could have turned out really bad for us."

"I'm alright. I do keep thinking about what could have happened, but I'm trying not to. I have to say, meeting Oliver last night sure made up for it. I really like him."

Harper laughed, "Really? I couldn't tell."

They both burst into laughter and for a little while, things felt like they used to, before a strange man, for reasons unknown to them, decided to target her family.

She decided to send a text to Noah asking him about lunch. He responded right away and said things were crazy right then, but he would hopefully see her that night. He said he would call her when he could.

Next, she tried her mother's cell again, and again it went to voicemail. Now, really worried, she decided to call her father's cell, and there was no answer. He has an old-fashioned flip phone, so she doubts he will even see that she called. They finished getting ready and decided to go down to the dining room and see if she couldn't locate her mother. Something was not right, but she didn't know what else to do. One more glance at her phone, and she realized she missed a text message from her mother about an hour ago. It must have come in when she was in the shower. Abby just wanted to let Harper know that she and Olivia were at the *Beau Rivage,* and they were to meet them there for lunch when they got up. She felt a little relieved, but still didn't like the fact that Abby wasn't answering her phone. They left the room and headed to the *Beau Rivage*, as instructed by her mother. Harper was then silently making excuses in her mind of all the reasons Abby wasn't answering her phone.

#

Everything happened so quickly. Seconds after Abby felt the hand on her mouth and her body being lifted up and pulled away from the bathroom, she was being pulled into another room that was close to the bathroom. Her mind was running wild with all sorts of ideas of what to do and fear of what might happen if she couldn't get away. She didn't get a look at the person because he caught her from behind. She knew it was a man because he kept mumbling something to her, but she had no idea what he was saying. He seemed frantic to make her understand something. He was also strong. Her first thought was of the man from the shuttle. He continued to hold his hand over her mouth, so she was unable to scream for help. She knew it was up to her to get out of the situation, hopefully unharmed.

She timed it right, and when he leaned into her to continue repeating something about being careful, she opened her mouth and bit down hard on his hand. For a moment, his hand dropped, and she fell back as hard as she could against him. They both toppled to the ground. At first, all she could think of was getting away, but within a few seconds that all changed. She wanted to hurt the man for attacking her. She reached for a broom stick leaning against the wall and with all her might, brought it down on top of his head. From there, she was able to push herself up and should have run out of there, but she didn't. It was as if something came over her and again, she felt the undeniable urge to hurt him. She began beating him with the broom stick until he stopped moving.

As quick as that feeling came over her, it left. Feeling confused and scared she reached for the door and ran out, running smack into Olivia.

Olivia was stunned for a moment, and then sprang into action, and they both ran from the hallway. Abby stopped for a moment to gather herself and then together they went to find a security guard to report what happened. The security guard called the police for help and when they arrived, they headed down the hall to the room that Abby had described to them.

Abby and Olivia followed the police and security guard to the hall and waited at the end while they cleared the area and entered the room. Someone grabbed Abby's shoulder and she screamed. She turned around ready to swing at whoever it was before she realized it was Harper. She had never been so happy to see her daughter. She grabbed her and held her close, trying to assure her everything was alright. Once the shock wore off, Abby explained to Harper what had happened and for what seemed like forever, they waited for the security guards to come back out of the hallway.

#

After running some distance, Griff and Tab finally got to a place where the traffic was moving at a better pace. They flagged down a local cop and Tab explained to him what was going on. They hurried into his car and headed towards the *Golden Nugget*. At that point, they were only a few miles away, but Griff welcomed the ride. He would like to think he could have continued and would've gotten there but he was not so sure. His legs were like jelly and his breathing was at an exhausted pace. He took this break to regroup and get ready to run when they got there. He was not sure what to do first. Should he head up to the room or look around the casino. He thought maybe she was in the spa, so he decided when they arrived; he was going to head there first. And since it was lunchtime, he asked Tab to cover all the restaurants.

They were in traffic again, but it was moving. Griff's phone rang and for a moment, he prayed it was Abby.

After looking at caller ID he realized it was Harper, and he picked up. Harper was with Abby and Olivia, and Griff listened to his daughter briefly explain what happened and where they were. At that point, the local police car carrying Griff and Tab was only a few blocks from the *Beau Rivage,* so he and Tab decided to jump out and run the rest of the way.

As he was running toward the *Beau Rivage*, Griff was flooded with emotions. *How can I face Abby when I wasn't there to protect her?* Harper had told Griff that Abby was fine, but he still couldn't stand the thought of what could have happened.

Tab was hoping that they had the guy in custody, and they would allow him to ask some questions. He didn't have jurisdiction in that state, but he usually got extended a courtesy from other counties. When Harper called, all she said was everyone was okay, the security guards were going to get the man, and that they were at the *Beau Rivage*. Tab was also hoping they called the Biloxi Police Department. Trey checked in and said he was still at the coliseum and that he still had the driver of the car with him. Trey confirmed that he would stay put until he heard from Tab.

Tab and Griff reached the *Beau Rivage* and headed straight to the back restaurant where Harper said they were. He had Abby in his sights and all he could think of was how beautiful she was and how much he loved her. He rushed to her side and was met with the same desperation he brought. Abby started to fill him in on the details of what happened to her, less the brutal way she beat the guy even after she was free to run away. That information, she decided, she would keep to herself. At least until she could understand what made her react that way.

Tab headed down the hallway where the attack occurred and where the officers were. As far as he could tell, there were two officers standing in the doorway speaking to someone in the room. As he approached, he flashed his badge and identified himself. The officer then moved aside and let him pass. Upon entering the room, another officer from inside the room looked at Tab with a puzzled look on his face. Tab canvassed the room with his eyes and saw exactly what the officer was confused about; there was no one else in the room. It appeared that there was a struggle of sorts with the room left ransacked. There was blood on the floor, splatters on the wall and a broom stick that lay nearby that also had blood on it.

"What the hell is going on here? Where's the suspect? I had clearance from your department to question him first. Who's in charge here?" Tab had a bad feeling about this.

The officer inside the room said he was in charge. "We arrived just about five minutes ago. We received a call from the casino of an attack on a woman in this room. When we got here, there was no one in the room. We spoke to the woman about the attack, and she directed us here. There appears to be some blood but by the look of things, the suspect was able to get up and walk away."

"What about video surveillance? Did anyone check it out?" Tab was grasping at straws. They had to get this guy soon.

"They are viewing it now, but there are no cameras in this hallway. We will only be able to see who comes in and who leaves. Hopefully, we can narrow it down and identify the suspect. The victim did say that when she headed down the hallway, she was alone. She had no idea where the man came from. It's possible he was in here waiting for her for a while, but how would he know she would come? I would venture to say he followed her, staying far enough back not to spook her."

Tab was sick knowing he had to walk back out there and tell Abby and Griff that there's no one in the room. He knew the pressure they both had been under since this started. And to be no closer than they were before would devastate them. When Griff asked him for his help with this case, he had no idea it was so serious. Someone was out there who was desperate to get to Abby and they didn't know why or what he had in store for her. When they got back home, he would make sure they had around the clock protection. He would not let his best friend down.

After the initial shock of the news, Griff and Abby agreed to go with Tab and find out what the video surveillance could tell them. First, Tab sat down with Abby to go over all the details of the attack. She assured him that her attacker was unconscious when she left him, possibly dead.

Abby recalled, "When he pulled me backwards, all I could think of was getting his hand from over my mouth. That's when I bit him and pushed all my weight backwards and we both went down. I think he was hurt from the fall, but I'm not sure. At that moment, I did see his face and it was the man I saw in the Dodge Dart. The funny thing was he kept rambling on about being careful and that he was trying to warn me about something. He said a lot of other stuff, but I was so scared that I was only focused on getting away. Once I was able to get to my feet, I reached for the broom and hit him a few times. When I realized he wasn't moving anymore, I ran for the door and didn't look back. I know he was hurt, so how did he disappear? I ran into Olivia when I came out and together, we ran to get the security guard. They called for help and within five minutes, the officers were here."

"The officers did say that they were right outside and were on the scene in about five minutes. Apparently with *Crusin the Coast* going on, they stepped up the security here. So, if that time frame is accurate, and I think it is, the suspect couldn't have been unconscious. Or, if he was, he recovered quickly. There could have been a second person, but you said he was alone, so I highly doubt he had an accomplice. We won't rule that out just yet. Let's go see that video and hopefully get some answer." Tab's frown suggested he wasn't too optimistic.

Abby still couldn't shake that horrible feeling of wanting to hurt that man. She was sure it was natural to want to hurt someone who intended on hurting you, but wouldn't your main objective be to just get away? She felt like she was in a nightmare, and it was just starting. She always wondered how she would react in a situation like that, and in all the different scenarios she played in her head, not once did she think her reaction would be anger and such hatred. That's what scared her the most; she never felt true hatred like that in her life, and she did not like the way it felt. *That has never been my nature. What's changed?* Abby pondered as she sat and waited.

CHAPTER 27

It was Sunday morning, and everyone was meeting for breakfast at the casino buffet at 9am. The events from the day before took all afternoon to sort through. The cameras did confirm it was Detective Hawkins who followed Abby into the hallway and attacked her. He had followed her from the time she arrived at the *Beau Rivage*. Abby thought it was all so crazy and was amazed at how it had unfolded in less than a few minutes. After the attack, in what they now knew was a utility closest, Abby ran from the room right into Olivia. They ran down the hall and seconds later, Detective Hawkins came out of the room and headed out into the crowd. She really thought he was knocked out and possibly dead. She still did not tell Griff or anyone else how she felt when she was beating him. Even though he got away, she was relieved to see that she didn't kill him. She wasn't sure she could live with that for the rest of her life.

One of the things that was bothering Abby the most was that feeling she got that maybe he didn't really want to attack her. Sure, he grabbed her and pulled her into that room but, looking back on it, she was starting to feel like he was just trying to tell her something. *It was like he was trying to warn me about something, but what could that be? And why would he go about it in that manner? He could have approached me with whatever it was he wanted to say, and just ask to speak with me.* She had all night to think about each time they crossed paths, that she was aware of, and determined that he did have many opportunities to talk to her. Apparently, he felt like she was not going to listen to him, but why? She was still so confused and wanted answers, but one thing had changed, she was not scared anymore. Her gut feeling was that he was not here to hurt her, but in his own strange way, to help her. Now, she had the impossible task of convincing Griff of that.

The previous afternoon, Trey had stayed with the suspect that was driving the Dodge Dart until Tab called. He told Trey to let the guy go, but to try and tail him. Jack went to the car and drove it back to the hotel. Not sure what they were going to do with it, but they didn't want to leave it on the street. The suspect walked all the way back to the Mall, found a wall, and sat down. From what Trey could see, there were other homeless people hanging out. It didn't appear that he was waiting to meet anyone except maybe a drug dealer. He reported that information to Tab and was instructed to hang tight while he sent someone to pick him up.

The previous night had to be the longest night in Griff's life. They tried to get some sleep, but he tossed and turned all night. He felt like he was living in a nightmare and couldn't wake up. *How did we let him slip away when we were so damn close*? He finally got out of bed around 5am and noticed Abby was sound asleep. He found that odd because usually something like this would bring on her panic attacks. But on the contrary, she looked so peaceful. It could be that she was so exhausted and was finally able to sleep. Whatever the reason, he was glad she was able to get some rest. After breakfast they were supposed to head home, and that was when he was going to add to her stress and tell her about the break in at their house. At least he took comfort in the fact that Tab was on top of that and promised to continue having 24-hour security at their house. Griff could only thank God for Tab, because he would hate to be going through all of this without a good friend's support.

At breakfast, Harper still seemed shaken up about what happened to her mother the previous afternoon. After all the commotion yesterday, she stayed close to her family. She was not letting her mother out of her sites again. She was beating herself up about sleeping late and not meeting her for breakfast. If anything would have happened to Abby, she would not be able to forgive herself. Thankfully, her mom kicked ass and was there to talk about it. She always knew her mother was a strong woman but at the same time she seemed fragile. She realized; *You never know what you would do in a situation like that.* She was sorry that she didn't get to meet up with Noah. She sent him a text that said she had family problems and that she needed to stay with them last night. He replied back that he understood and that he was actually tied up with something for work. They agreed to touch base when they get back home.

A smile crossed Harper's face and it was all because for the first time in a long time, she really liked someone. Noah seemed to feel the same way, and Harper was excited to see where their relationship would go. She knew her mother would be even more excited than her. She and Henly were dressing for breakfast and packing up everything so that right after breakfast, they could get on the road. Her parents were leaving then, and she wanted to follow them home. Her father was supposed to tell her mother about what happened the other night. She was glad she had her own car. Her mom was going to go ballistic when she found out Harper went to the house after being told not to. Harper knew her mother would ring her phone, yelling at her the minute she found out. At least she had almost two hours in the car to calm down. Besides, her mother was supposed to stay with Olivia at all times and she didn't, so how can she blame Harper? Harper knew she needed to deal with having gone to the house, but really, she was just ready to get home and focus on Noah, and the upcoming Halloween party. She loved this time of the year.

"Are we ready to get on the road," Griff asked Abby and Harper after breakfast. He had been a little anxious that morning because he had to tell his wife what happened at home, and he was not looking forward to it. He was just ready to get it over with. He didn't like to keep things from her, but he knew that was the right thing to do in this case. Tab and Trey left early that morning to get home and secure the house for them. Olivia and Jack joined them for breakfast and were also leaving with them.

"I'm ready. We packed the car before breakfast. I guess we will see you at home." Harper kissed her parents and Olivia and Jack and got in her car. Henly made her rounds too and got in the car. Griff winked at Harper and told her to drive safely.

Olivia hugged Abby and asked, "Are y'all driving straight home?"

"Yes. I am ready to get home and start focusing on Halloween again. I really hope we can find Detective Hawkins soon, because I have a lot of errands to run and Griff's not going to leave my side until they catch him." Abby hugged her best friend in return, and Olivia and Jack got in their car.

After the stressful events of the weekend, everyone was ready to be home. They all thought for sure that they had a good chance of catching up with the detective there, so they are all leaving a little disappointed. Abby put her seat back a little, ready to relax and reflect on the events. Griff really hated to do it to her, but he had to tell her what happen before she goes to sleep.

He started with, "I can't believe this guy got away. I really thought we had him. How are you holding up? I know it's been a stressful weekend."

Abby didn't open her eyes when she responded. "I'm fine. I just want to get home and forget about this and enjoy the rest of the season."

"About that, I have something to tell you. Just know that there was no reason for you to know any of this until now."

Abby sat up and stared at her husband. The sound of his voice was making her nervous. *What is he talking about?* Abby thought but didn't say. "Just spit it out. What is it?"

"Well, Friday night after we left, Harper and Henly went to the house to get some clothes for the weekend."

"You gotta be kidding me. I told her not to go to the house alone. What is wrong with that girl?" Abby reached for her phone to call her daughter.

Griff stopped her. "Wait there's more. When they got to the house, they both went up to Harpers room. After a few minutes in the house, they heard a noise downstairs. They dialed 911 and ran out of the house. They hid by the neighbors until the police arrived, but they saw a man run out of the house towards the woods. The officers contacted Tab and he called Harper. She asked him to call me and not to upset you until she was safely on her way here. Even though the man was wearing a hoodie and shielded his face from the cameras, Tab feels strongly that it was Detective Hawkins."

Abby just stared at her husband for what seemed like forever. Then she reached over and slapped him across the face. Her first thought was to punch him in his face, but she was able to contain herself and delivered a slap instead. There was that feeling again, the feeling of such hatred and anger. She was so mad that he kept this from her. It definitely upset her, but never before had she wanted to hurt Griff. Sure, he had angered her in the past and she wanted to rip his head off, but this was different. She began to cry uncontrollably and her whole body started to shake.

Griff pulled the car over right away and rushed to her side of the car. He opened her door and grabbed her and held her so tight she could hardly breathe.

"It's alright Abby. Harper is fine. That's why I didn't feel like I wanted to tell you about it Friday. You were having such a good day I didn't want to ruin it for you. And there was nothing you could do about it anyway. Please forgive me Abby and please stop crying."

She wanted to forgive him, she really did, but at the same time she wanted him to suffer. *How could he have kept this from me? Why was he treating me like a baby? Did he think I was too weak to handle it? I don't need anyone trying to protect me by lying to me.* No, she was not ready to forgive him. She pushed him away, gathered herself and put her seatbelt back on.

All she said was, "Please take me home."

Griff had a puzzled look on his face. He couldn't believe she was behaving this way. Sure, she could always get really mad, and they had their fights, but she always got over things quickly. That was one of the things he admired most about her.

All he could say was, "Fine" and slammed her door shut. They drove the rest of the way home in silence. Abby had her eyes closed but he could tell she was not sleeping. He was really sorry he kept this from her, but he didn't lie. He had never lied to his wife, and it really made him mad that she would say that.

His mind slipped to the weekend events. Driving in silence gave him a lot of time to hash over everything. Tab talked about going to Summit and looking for some connection between the old lady Abby bought the stick from and Detective Hawkins. It was a long shot but worth the trip. He was going to call Tab when he got home and see when they could go, the sooner, the better for Griff. Besides, if Abby wanted to stay mad at him, he'd rather not be home. A little space between them was probably good and maybe it would give her time to come to her senses. At that thought, he had a strange feeling that this was only the beginning.

CHAPTER 28

It had been a week since they returned from Biloxi and Abby still couldn't shake the intense feeling of anger she was feeling towards Griff. She realized that he was just trying to protect her and not ruin her weekend. She knew he didn't actually lie to her, but it felt like a betrayal. And that was something she could not forgive; not yet anyway.

Since they came home things had been crazy. Not knowing where the Detective was, and if he was the only one stalking them, had everyone on edge. Today was the first time Abby felt somewhat normal in a long time. Griff had returned to his routine and went into the office. She decided to get back to her walking with hopes of getting back to her old self. With everything going on, everyone was trying to be extra careful and not go anywhere alone. Olivia was on her way over now to join Abby for her morning walk. She had been there for Abby from the beginning and continued to prove just how great of a friend she was.

Everything was quiet and it turned out to be a beautiful morning for a walk. They had their usual conversation and Abby continued to feel more relaxed. They had been together so much lately that after the first few miles, conversation slowed down. She began to reflect on everything going on and started to feel agitated again.

Olivia noticed Abby's silence and tried to reassure her, "Everything's going to be alright Ab. Griff and Tab are going to find this guy soon and..."

Before she could finish her sentence, Abby cut her off and with a look Olivia had never seen before said, "How do you know that Olivia? You don't know anything. This man could be following us right now or worse following Harper. He was in my house. You don't know how it feels to have a stranger in your house doing God knows what. So, don't tell me it's going to be alright when you can't know that!" Her voice rose with each sentence and before she knew it, she was yelling at her best friend. Abby knew she shouldn't be yelling at her, but it felt good. "I just wish everyone would stop treating me like a fragile little girl because I'm not. When Detective Hawkins attacked me, I knocked him down and could have run away. But instead I picked up that broom stick and hit him again and again. I wanted to hurt him, and I did! I'm only sorry he got away. I can take care of myself!"

Olivia stopped mid-step, with her mouth open, and stood there, horrified. *Who is this person yelling at me?* Never in all the years they had been friends had Abby even raised her voice at Olivia. And she didn't stop. She went on for a few more minutes and then turned and walked off leaving Olivia stunned. She waited for a few moments, gathered herself and then went after Abby. Something was going on with her friend and she was scared that if she didn't find out what, and soon, she may lose her.

When she reached the house, Abby went straight upstairs and got in the shower. She didn't want to talk to Olivia or try to explain why she yelled at her. She didn't know why herself. She just wanted to find this guy and get on with her life.

Olivia didn't try to talk to Abby. She decided to head home and give her some time to calm down. The last thing she wanted to do was upset her more than she already was. On the drive home, Olivia replayed the episode over and over again, trying to pinpoint exactly when the conversation changed and what triggered it. But she couldn't seem to find a trigger. It was as if she just snapped and became angry, like she was suddenly someone else. Now the big question was, should she tell Griff? Things had been strained between Griff and Abby since Biloxi.

She decided to go home and sit on it for a while. Even though everything going on was directed towards Abby and her family, Olivia was feeling the stress too. Maybe they both just needed some down time. She didn't have anything planned for the day, so she decided to take an early nap. She'll talk to Abby later.

Olivia's phone rang and she jumped up out of a dead sleep. She looked at the clock and saw that it was already 11:30am. She slept for several hours. She grabbed her phone and said hello.

"Hey Liv, I was thinking about going to grab some lunch and getting started on the Halloween preparations. Are you in?"

Olivia stood quiet for what seemed like several minutes trying to understand what was going on. *Is this a joke?* Abby sounded as if nothing happened.

"Liv, can you hear me? Are you there?"

"I'm here. What did you say?" Olivia was still reeling from shock.

Abby repeated, "Let's go have lunch and go to Party City. Halloween is coming quickly, so we need to get started. I'll meet you at Gattuso's in an hour." The line went dead, and she was gone.

Olivia laid there confused for a while. She considered pulling the blanket over her head and going back to sleep. Surely, she was justified in feeling angry with Abby. No one could blame her for being mad and just not showing up. After laying there for another few minutes, she went up-stairs to get ready. Maybe no one could blame her, but she would blame herself. Her friend was going through something, and she knew if it were reversed, Abby would be there for her.

Gattuso's was always packed at that time of the day. Olivia looked around for Abby but didn't see her. She got a table and ordered a drink. They might have to get an Uber driver after the day she was having. One drink might not be enough.

Abby arrived and looked so calm and happy. She actually looked happy.

Olivia stood up and gave Abby a hug, and asked, "How are you feeling?"

Abby innocently replied, "I'm feeling great. How about you?"

Olivia's heart began to pound. Abby's behavior suggested that she didn't remember what happened earlier that morning. *How could this be happening?* She started to panic a little. *What am I supposed to do? Should I bring it up or just play along?* She decided to play along for now. This was serious and she wanted to handle it correctly. Later, she would reach out to someone who specialized in things like this, and hopefully find the best way to handle it.

Olivia picked up her drink, raised it and said, "I'm on my way to feeling great; care to join me?"

They spent a few hours laughing and enjoying their lunch. When they finally left the restaurant both women were completely relaxed and at ease. They were so at ease, that they forgot everything that had been going on lately and failed to notice they were being followed. Detective Hawkins was hot on their trail once again.

#

Though he kept a safe distance, Detective Hawkins continued to follow the two women. He had to find a way to get to Abby and make her understand what was going on. He learned from Biloxi that it was not going to be easy. Her reaction to him grabbing her was alarming. Most people would try to get away. She exhibited the exact behavior he was trying to warn her about, which meant it was already starting. All he wanted to do was warn her. She needed to know what she was dealing with before it was too late. He refused to let this happen all over again. *This time,* he thought, *things will turn out differently.*

He had to admit, following Abby had been challenging. He had never met someone who was on the go so much. Where he's from, tailing someone was much easier. Life went at a lot slower pace, and people tended to stay home more often. He and his colleagues did a lot of this kind of work, but it usually entailed sitting in your car for hours and hours, bored to death. Sometimes they were called to McComb, Mississippi and that was usually more challenging, but it still didn't come close to this area. In Gretna, things were so busy. Crime was relatively low but trying to follow someone without being noticed was difficult. Especially this time of year. Since it was fall, people were out walking around.

Luckily, Abby did frequent the same few restaurants, so that made things a little bit easier. He was surprised when she left the house earlier that day. It had been a week since their encounter, and this was the first time she had gone out. She did go out for her usual walk that morning, but he thought it better to wait until she officially left the house to start following her. Since they returned home, there had been around the clock security at the house. He was not sure if Abby realized, but she had a tail on her since she left the house. Griff and Abby Stewart were heavily guarded these days and he couldn't blame them. The only problem was, they had no idea what the real threat was or how to protect themselves from it. All the security in the world couldn't protect them from what was coming from within. That was why he needed to get to her soon. Time was running out.

#

Abby asked Olivia, "What do you think about this?"

She had on a white lab coat and a wig. Olivia turned and began to giggle.

"That looks great, but are you going to be Morgus or Chopsley? The coat is perfect, but it needs to be a little more worn and dirtier. We can take care of that later. The wig is perfect. I haven't decided what we are going to be this year. Since you are decorating your house like a laboratory, I was thinking maybe Frankenstein and Bride of Frankenstein. What do you think?"

Now Abby was giggling. "That's a great idea. I think Jack should be the Bride of Frankenstein and you should be Frankenstein."

"Now you sound like Griff. I don't know if Jack would go for that. It would be funny though." Neither one of them knew exactly why, but they begin to laugh hysterically. Abby thought, it was probably from the drinks at lunch, or the stress. She didn't really care why; it was just nice to laugh like that again. She and Olivia were always laughing and that was part of why they were so close. Laughter was good for the soul. Abby considered Olivia family and felt so grateful to have her in her life.

After they recovered from laughing, Abby got the strangest feeling, as if something wasn't right. The kind of feeling that makes your hair stand on end, as if something bad was happening. But as far as Abby could tell, not much of anything was going on. She was just enjoying her day with her best friend. *Am I missing something? Did something happen that I don't know about?* Abby stepped aside and grabbed her phone to dial Harper. Her daughter answered in her usual groggy voice for that time of the day. She was obviously still sleeping. She told her she was just checking up and hurried off the phone. Next, she touched base with Alex and Griff, and both were alright. She was not sure how, but she knew something was coming and it was not going to be good. She looked up to find Olivia staring at her.

"Are you alright? You look like you saw a ghost."

"I'm fine. I just had a strange feeling that something was wrong, but I guess I'm a little paranoid these days. Let's go to the Spirit Halloween store and see what they have there." And with that, Abby started walking towards the door.

That was it for Olivia. She decided that when she got home, she was going to call Griff and fill him in. Maybe he could talk to Abby and possibly encourage her to go see her therapist. She knew her best friend extremely well and she was acting way too weird these days. She needed help and Olivia was going to make sure she got it one way or another.

CHAPTER 29

SEPTEMBER 2007

When he arrived on the scene, all he could think was, *Not again!* Things had been quiet for ten years. He thought it was all over, and that they had put a stop to the killings the last time this happened in 1997. He put a call into his captain, so that he could get to the bottom of things.

He heard a voice from the back of the house, "Detective Hawkins can you come here please?" He walked through the kitchen to a small room in the back. It appeared to be a mud room, but it was covered in blood, not mud. The room appeared to be empty, but it was clear something had happened in there.

The 911 call was from a woman who found her neighbor running in circles in the street, hysterical and covered in blood. When the police arrived, they found the woman in the street, called an ambulance, and then called for back up to go check out her house. That was where Detective Hawkins came in. He and his rookie partner arrived just as the ambulance was pulling away and found the front door to the distraught woman's house wide open.

He didn't know why or how but he immediately knew that this case was related to the others. Detective Hawkins felt that he had to be connected somehow with all the cases because he was always the one closest and on call when the murders happened? Clearly, that was no coincidence.

They found a body in the back yard right outside the mud room. And like all the others it was beaten beyond recognition. They combed the rest of the house and the grounds and thankfully there were no other bodies. If he had to guess, the hysterical woman running in the street was the murderer. He did find one thing very odd about the scene, no murder weapon. *How could that be? There was nothing to suggest that the woman had gone anywhere after the murder, other than running in circles in the street. The murder weapon used in the other murders had been in the evidence room since 1997.* Somehow, it made its way into each of those people's lives with nothing in common. *So, how could this case be related to the others if the murder weapon is locked up?* Maybe he was wrong, and it was not a related case, but it sure felt like it.

Just then, his phone rang, and it was the captain. When he called earlier, Detective Hawkins asked him to confirm that the walking stick used in the last case as the murder weapon was still in the evidence room. To his surprise, it was gone. The captain said they searched the entire place, and it was nowhere to be found and he offered no explanation. Could it be that the woman outside was in possession of the stick, and it was once again used in a gruesome murder? That would be a long shot, but he didn't rule it out. Everything about those cases were so bizarre and each one surprised him a little bit more than the last. He's not willing to give up though. He was determined to find the murder weapon and then he was going to launch his own investigation into the disappearance of the last murder weapon. If it turned out to be one in the same, he would find out. That was his area of expertise.

CHAPTER 30

2017

Both Harper and Noah had been so busy since they returned from Biloxi after *Crusin' the Coast* they hardly had any time to see each other. Although she missed seeing him in person, she still saw him since they Face-Timed each other every day. One of the things taking up so much of her time was her mother. She had gotten really scared when her mother didn't answer her phone in Biloxi, and now she felt like she wanted to stay close to home for a while, at least until they caught this guy. And it was only a few weeks away from their annual Halloween party. All hands on deck for that event.

Her mother always threw these elaborate parties. When Harper was a child, they would have hayrides, apple bobbing and even a Haunted House. They would invite her entire class and their families. Then, later that evening when all the kids left, the real party would start. Her mom would have music, food, and spirits of course. She would always allow Harper to stay up later than usual and see the guest come in their costumes. It was fun to try and figure out who was who. Since they were older, the kid's parties have been cancelled. They all enjoyed one big party including Gabrielle, her niece and E.R. her nephew. Now, E.R. is 18 and invited a lot of his own friends to the party, just like Harper.

She had planned to invite Noah to the party when she talked to him that night. She was hoping he would say yes, not only to the party but to maybe coordinating their costumes. She had never done that before. Well, not with a boy anyway. She and Henly used to always dress alike. Her last boyfriend, Ted, thought dressing up was for kids. He was immature and always worried about what other people thought. That relationship only lasted through high school, and thankfully, he ended it when he left for college. Looking back, he was just someone to pass the time with. She had some wonderful memories from her childhood and high school years, thanks to her mother. That was why it was so important that she helped her mom out this year and participated in all the preparations.

Since Abby got home earlier from lunch with Olivia, she felt like a new person. After the morning she and Olivia had, shopping and laughing, she began to feel like her old self again. The party was coming up quickly, so she jumped right into decorating.

Right now, Abby had Harper on decorating duty. Her mother called her earlier waking her up and Harper recalled that she sounded weird. She was usually aggravated that Harper slept late, but that wasn't it. She sounded stressed and out of control. After spending the night at Henly's, Harper decided to get up and go over to the house to see what was going on. That was how she found herself stuck decorating, but at least it was a nice day.

Every year they decorated the outside of the house for fall. They used pumpkins, hay and had yellow and orange garland hanging everywhere. Specifically for Halloween, they transformed the inside of the garage into whatever theme her mom picked for that year. This year, it was going to be a laboratory and her parents were going as Morgus the Magnificent and Chopsley. It was going to be an interesting one.

She wanted to do some research on costumes related to a laboratory before she talked to Noah. He may be more willing if she had a few ideas to throw out there. It was break time anyway, so it was a good time to look on-line. She went to grab her iPad and a snack. This year's party was going to be so good; she could feel it. As she sat down her phone rang, and it was Noah. He must have been on a break at work because he didn't FaceTime her.

Harper answered her phone on the second ring, "Hey Noah, surprised to hear from you this morning. Are you at work?"

"Actually, yes, I am. I'm calling to tell you that I have to go out of town for work again. Something just came up and I just found out we are leaving in an hour. It's the same case we've been working on. I'm not sure how long we'll be gone or if I'll get a chance to call you tonight. I wanted to make sure I got to talk to you at least once today. Harper, I wanted you to know that I think about you all day and can't wait to see you again."

Harper tried her best not to scream with happiness, "I think about you all day too. I understand this is your job, but please be safe and come home soon. Hey Noah, I wanted to ask you something when we FaceTime later, but I guess that might not happen. My family has a big Halloween party every year and I was hoping you would come with me this year." She held her breath waiting for his response.

"I would love to be your date Harper. I'll get the details from you later; I have to go now. I'll call you as soon as I can. See you soon."

Abby walked into the kitchen to find Harper jumping up and down with excitement. It made her smile to see her daughter so happy. And without asking, she was sure it had something to do with Noah. She was wondering what was going on with them lately but knew better than to ask.

"What's going on in here?" Abby asked with a grin on her face that suggested she already knew.

Harper jumped at the sound of her mother's voice

"Nothing much, what are you up to mom?" She was not ready to discuss Noah with her mom. Her mother always made a big deal out of everything, and Harper was enjoying the slow pace at which her relationship with Noah was progressing.

"That didn't look like nothing to me. How are you coming with the decorating? Olivia and I spent a few days trying to get what we needed, but I'm sure we missed something."

"We might need some more pumpkins. That's my favorite part of all the decorations for fall, the pumpkins. I love the scarecrows too. Oh, I guess I love it all." Harper got up and headed back outside.

Abby yelled after her daughter, "Dad is going out of town today so could you please stay close to home?" Harper nodded.

I guess that conversation is over, Abby said to herself. Griff called a while ago to say that they were heading to Summit to try and find a connection between that store and Detective Hawkins. They all realized they were grasping at straws but hoped for some link between the two.

"The old lady... The old lady...The old lady," Abby stopped suddenly when she realized she was having another moment of intrusive thoughts about an old lady. She had been hearing those words come into her head for a couple of days, but she had no idea what they meant. She was hoping for some conversation with Harper to occupy her mind but that didn't work. She had to admit, the internal dialog about the old lady was driving her crazy.

A few days ago, Griff suggested Abby call her therapists, Dr. Weber, just to talk to her about everything going on. At the time, she thought he was overreacting, and she became angry with him. She would never admit it to him, but maybe that's exactly what she needed. She decided to call for an appointment.

Of course, they couldn't get her in to see the doctor until next Thursday. They had asked if it was an emergency, but she told them no. If the intrusive thoughts about the old lady didn't improve by the following day, she thought she would probably call them back. She decided she would just focus on staying busy. With Griff gone, she didn't have to worry about dinner, so she decided to take a quick nap. A nap usually made her feel better. She hoped she would be able to fall asleep.

Suddenly, Harper was outside and heard a scream from inside. She ran to check on her mother and saw that she was sleeping on the sofa in the living room, and she seemed to be having a terrible dream. She wasn't sure if she should wake her mom up or let her sleep. Harper knew her mom could really use some rest but wondered if this was even restful sleep if she was screaming in the middle of it. Since Harper was in the room, Abby seemed to have calmed down, and wasn't as restless. She was still moving around and mumbling, but she was slowly calming down. Harper decided to just sit in the chair next to the sofa and wait a little longer before waking her. Most of what she was saying sounded like gibberish but every now and then she could make out a word or two. "Careful, old lady, look, be, within, Harper, Dodge, darkness." Nothing was making any sense. After about twenty minutes, Abby was quiet, and Harper ended up falling asleep beside her.

Abby stood stunned, and after a quick glance around, tried to wrap her head around what she was seeing. She tried to remember the sequence of events. One minute she was lying on the sofa and the next minute she was being pulled into a closet. She kept hearing a voice say, *"Be Careful, Look Within,"* but what did that mean? Someone had their hand over her mouth and their arm tightly around her waist, and she couldn't scream. *"Old Lady, Old Lady,"* echoed in her ear. At that moment, Abby slipped into a full-blown panic attack, and she shook in rage as she realized she had to get away from the person that grabbed her. She threw her weight back into the person behind her, and they both fell back against the closet wall. With lightning speed, she felt the urge to hurt the person fill her stomach, and she began kicking and hitting with as much force as she could muster. She grabbed him by the throat and realized it was Detective Hawkins. *Why won't you leave me alone?* Abby wondered angrily. She thought about how he had made her life so miserable lately and it had to stop. All she could think of was that he would not be walking out of there! They struggled for a while and then she felt a sharp slap across her face. She fumbled backwards and realized she was in her living room on the floor.

Harper was on the floor beside her, gasping for air and when she caught her breath yelled, "What the hell, mom? What are you doing?"

"What do you mean what am I doing? Why are you on the floor?" Abby was so confused.

"Don't you remember what just happen? You were having a nightmare, and you were screaming and talking in your sleep. I heard you from outside and ran in to see what was going on. After a while, you settled down and I fell asleep, also. Next thing I know, you were on top of me yelling and trying to strangle me. What were you dreaming about? You better go and get some help because you are losing it!" Harper stomped out the room and headed to the kitchen to get something to drink. Her neck was killing her. Her mother really scared her. Thank God she woke up when Harper slapped her because who knows what could have happened. That woman on top of her was definitely not her mother, and that really scared Harper. She wished her dad were home. She wanted to call him, but there was really nothing he could do now, and she didn't want to worry him while he was out of town. But she didn't want to leave her mother alone and at the same time, didn't want to be alone with her. She never thought she would ever feel afraid of her own mother.

She decided to call her sister, Alex. She had been so busy lately with Gabrielle and gymnastics, but Harper knew she would want to know what happened. She quickly filled Alex in over the phone and Alex said she would be right over. Finn would be home early enough that day to get Gabby from school and take her to practice.

Just as she hung up the phone, her mother came into the kitchen. She looked awful. Abby was always a pretty woman. She very seldom wore makeup because she has a natural beauty to her. When Harper looked at her mom as she walked into the kitchen, she saw circles under her eyes and her usual glow was gone. She was staring at Harper with a blank expression. There was darkness in her eyes. She appeared to be confused, scared and sad all at the same time.

Harper rushed over to her mother, wrapped her arms around her and tried to comfort her. Abby began to cry, and she and Harper just stood in the kitchen holding each other for a good long while. Harper chuckled to herself thinking how strange this was and that it was usually the other way around, her mother comforting her. Before long, Alex came bursting through the door and grabbed the both of them. The three stayed there for the better part of an hour, holding each other tight without saying a word. They were afraid to let go and face what was happening. Sooner or later, they would have to let go, but for now they held on.

After a few hours of being together, they decided it was best for her mother to take a sleeping pill and go to bed. Harper ran out to pick up some food, and after they all ate, Abby went upstairs to go to bed. Harper and Alex took turns checking on her throughout the evening.

Harper filled Alex in on the details of what happened earlier. She still couldn't believe that her mother had it in her to attack that way. Alex just sat listening and was mortified by the details. Their mother was not a violent person. She smacked them a few times growing up but only when they deserved it. She and their Dad were both very easy-going people. It seemed like darkness was taking over and looming down on her family and she was not going to stand by and let it happen.

CHAPTER 31

Summit was bustling with people enjoying the weather. Tab, Trey, and Griff had to park on a side street and walk down to the main street. Tab was on high alert trying to assess the scene as they walked. This threat against his best friend Griff and his family had him disturbed. He thought it would be simple to catch the guy and find out what he wanted, but he had proven to be a real expert at not being found. He was probably hiding in plain sight.

Tab was not surprised, because ever since they identified him as a retired Detective, he knew it would be difficult to catch him. He was still beating himself up for letting him slip through their fingers in Biloxi. From what Abby described and the amount of blood in that closet, it was a miracle he got away. Now they were back in Summit, following a hunch Griff had that this all started when he and Abby visited a store here back in September. They were not sure what to even look for, but Griff was adamant about finding a connection there.

They walked up one side of the strip looking for the store. Griff and Abby visited several of them that day and he was not sure which ones. They walked into each store and looked around. They were all full of used furniture and stuff some considered antiques, but the stores all looked alike to Griff. Frustrated, he took a deep breath and went to the next store.

It was getting to be lunch time and they were getting hungry. Griff spoke to Abby earlier and she was at home. There was something odd in her voice, but he couldn't think of that now. The sooner he got his answers there, the sooner he could get home. He spoke to Harper, and she said she would be home shortly, so he was glad about that.

"Let's take a break and have lunch. Then we can check out the stores on the other side of the street. I really want to get home to Abby." Griff headed to a restaurant on the corner.

"Something's not adding up. I don't know what it is, but I get the feeling we should be looking for someone who knows Detective Hawkins. He's from this area. Maybe we should run a check on who owns these stores and if he is connected somehow. Trey, can you get on that after lunch?" Tab sounded agitated looking at Griff who had a bleak, pained look on his face. It was hard to see his friend like that.

Trey nodded and said, "I'm on it. I'll let you know what I find." He hadn't known Griff or Tab for long but had already grown fond of both of them. He had a lot to learn about the field from Tab, but he was good with the internet. He was more than happy to go to the truck and do some research. The quicker they could find that connection, the quicker things would move.

Tab, Trey, and Griff were finishing up lunch when Griff suddenly had the feeling that he had been in that exact spot, which quickly increased his anxiety. He realized that he was sitting in the exact restaurant he and Abby ate at the day they came to Summit to buy the walking stick. With that realization, he looked up to notice the exact store they were looking for all day, right across the street.

"That's it!" Griff pointed to a store across the street. It was called Second Chances.

Griff ran out of the restaurant and Tab followed. He yelled, "Griff slow down! Take a breath. Let's not alarm anyone by running in the store. Remember, we want to get them to talk to us."

Griff, heeding Tab's advice, stopped to regroup. He was standing by the store's front door and remembered the feeling he had when he was last there. He told Tab, "Abby was looking for a walking stick and couldn't find the one she wanted. As we were leaving the store that day, I was in front of Abby, and she called out to me that she found one. When I turned around, the hair on my arms stood up. It felt like something evil passed through my body. At the time, I let it go and went to the car while Abby paid. When she came to the car, she said a little old lady came from the back of the store with the perfect stick. We drove home and I never thought about that feeling again, until I told you about it and now again as we stand here. Abby described the 'Old Lady' as short with grey hair and really old. That shouldn't be too hard to find."

"Let's go find this lady."

They walked in the store and decided to split up, each taking a different side of the store to check things out. There were a few people browsing around but overall it was quiet. After going down every isle, Tab and Griff met at the front register. There were two women behind the register, one that appeared to be in her 50's and the other not more than 30 years old. They didn't see anyone else in the store, especially not someone fitting Abby's description.

Walking up to the register Tab asked the older of the two women, "I wonder if you can help me. We are looking for the elderly woman who works here. She sold my friend's wife a walking stick and we would like to talk to her if we could."

"I'm sorry, who are you looking for?" The woman looked confused.

"One of your employees, an elderly woman, grey hair, short. It was about three weeks ago."

"I'm sorry but there is no one fitting that description working here."

Griff stepped in eager to find answers. "Ma'am, I was here a few weeks ago with my wife and we were looking for a walking stick."

Before he could continue, the younger woman stepped up and said, "Yes, I remember you and your wife. She asked me about walking sticks, and I showed her this barrel here full of them. She explained that she wanted something old and unique, and I told her I didn't think we had anything like that at the time. She left the counter and headed for the door with you. I checked out the next customer and the next thing I knew she was back at the counter with an old walking stick. I thought she went back in and looked around herself. Like I said, I didn't think we had one but look around, there's so much stuff in here. I was surprised, but she was so happy to find the stick I didn't give it any more thought."

Griff interrupted her asking," What about the old lady?"

"I'm sorry we can't be more help, but my mother and I are the only people working here. We opened the store last year and have never hired anyone else. Business is just not that good for more than two of us," responded the younger of the two women.

Tab grabbed Griff by the arm, and they stepped aside to talk about this.

"Are you sure this is the store. I know the woman remembers you, but I have to ask."

Griff, feeling frustrated answered Tab a little sharper than he intended to. "Of course, I'm sure! And I know Abby didn't go back in the store. Someone came to her with that stick. This doesn't make sense. Let's go find out what Trey came up with."

Trey had always been a wiz with the computer. He was glad he could finally use his skills to help the guys out. He knew he was just an intern, but aside from learning, he had a lot to offer. It didn't take him long to find the name of the owners of the store. Tammy Schoust and her daughter, Lauren Picou, purchased the store on February 11, 2016. They moved to Summit from Georgia, just a few months earlier. As far as he could tell they didn't have any relations in the area. The previous ownership was where he was running into trouble. He decided when they get back home, he was going to run a full search and try to find out who the original owners were.

Griff and Tab headed back to the truck empty handed. They were hoping Trey came up with something. Griff stopped to call Abby and let her know they were heading back. Her phone rang and rang and finally went to voicemail. Maybe she was in the shower or something. He decided to wait a few minutes and try again.

When Griff reached the truck, Trey was filling in Tab on what he had found out about the current store owners, and they were discussing a new plan of action. They filled him in and decided their next course of action was to trace back the history of that store. They got on I55 and headed home.

Griff dialed Abby's phone again once they were on the road. This time Alex answered.

"Hello, Dad its Alex." His oldest daughter was whispering into the phone.

"Alex, where is your mother?"

"She's sleeping. She wasn't feeling well so Harper called me to come over. She's fine, she just looks exhausted. We talked her into taking a sleeping pill and going to bed. I decided to stay over, and I made Harper stay too. When are you coming home?"

Griff immediately kicked into high alert. When he left that morning, Abby was fine. And why would Harper call Alex if Abby just needed sleep. He knew she'd been overcome with weariness lately and he was thinking that he probably shouldn't have left her today. He could tell from Alex's voice that she was not telling him everything. And he knew her well. She was not going to give him any more information. She had always been able to keep a secret and knew when to keep her mouth shut. Now Harper on the other hand would've spilled it already. He was sure that was why Alex answered and not Harper.

"I'm on my way home now. If there's no traffic, we should be there around 7pm. Call me if you need anything. And Alex, thanks for taking care of mom." Griff chuckled and added, "And Harper, too. Love you honey. See you soon."

Griff hung up the phone and knew he was in for another long ride home. Griff was really starting to hate leaving town. He felt useless when he was so far away but, sometimes he had to go. And good thing he went because the women in the store remembered him and Abby. If nothing else, they learned there was no old lady working there. *Could she have just been a customer who saw the stick and heard Abby asking for one?* It was possible, but not likely. Griff's head hurt from trying to analyze the situation they were in. Nothing made sense. It was completely exhausting. He decided to lean back and try to take a nap. Lord knows what he's going to find when he gets home.

#

Abby slept sound for a few hours but found herself wide awake. She laid there for a while trying to decide if she should let the girls know she was up or just lay there and reflect on the current episode. *Did I really attack Harper? What was that about?* She realized she was dreaming, but it seemed so real. She was beginning to feel anxious again, so she jumped out of bed. She headed down the stairs to find both Harper and Alex sleeping on the sofa with a Netflix series on the television. She left them sleeping and went into the kitchen to fix herself something to drink. A tall glass of wine would be nice, but something told her that was probably not a good idea right now.

She grabbed a bottle of water from the fridge and stared out the window. What she really needed was to go for a nice walk. She went into the laundry room, grabbed her walking stick and off she went. She knew the girls would flip out if they knew she left the house, but she'll be back before they even wake up. It was already six o'clock, so she didn't have a lot of time and she had her cell phone if she needed something.

It was a lovely evening for a walk. Abby had been walking for about fifteen minutes and she felt good. It was just what she needed. Lately, it took a lot of exercise to get rid of all of her anxious energy. It had been a little over a week and there hadn't been any major incidences. Maybe she scared Detective Hawkins when she fought back. He probably thought she was an easy target. Little did he know that Abby could take care of herself. And, if he even tried to mess with her daughter's, he was going to see and even more aggressive side of her, she was sure of it.

As if almost on cue, someone grabbed Abby from behind and began to aggressively drag her towards the woods. All she could think was, *You've got to be kidding me!* Then, she quickly thought, *You are not getting me in the woods!* Again, she fell backwards with all her weight and they both tumbled to the ground. Abby thought to herself, *That always works.*

For a moment, she was stunned when she realized that it was him. Detective Hawkins was attacking her again. This time he moved backwards and began to try to talk to her.

"Mrs. Stewart, please wait! Listen to me. I have to warn you, especially now that I know what is happening and why. Please listen to me! I finally have the answers."

Something snapped again in Abby and all she wanted to do was hurt him. She raised the stick and started beating him. With every strike she thought, *If I don't hurt him, he's going to hurt me.* In the back of her mind, she tried reasoning with herself that he only wanted to talk, but she couldn't stop. She continued to strike him again and again until she was tackled to the ground.

Oh my God, he has an accomplice! Her mind was still racing, but she knew she had to fight. She swung the stick again and hit her assailant in the leg, dropping him to the ground. She lost her grip on the stick and realized she needed to run. She just had to make it back home.

When she reached her house, she ran into the back door. She turned to run into the kitchen and ran into her two daughters.

"Mom! Mom! Stop! What are you doing? Where were you?" Alex was looking at this person in front of her and barely recognized her.

Abby pushed Alex aside and ran to the closet. She was looking for her gun to finally put an end to this mess. *They'll die if they come after me again,* Abby heard her internal dialogue utter. The gun was gone, and Abby was stumped for a moment. Before long, she ran back to the laundry room and grabbed one of Griff's golf clubs. *This will do!* She stood there waiting for them to come through the door.

CHAPTER 32

While Abby stood ready to attack at the back door, sirens began to wail in the distance. Alex and Harper were standing behind their mother, not knowing what to do. She was displaying disturbing behavior and both girls were scared. *What should we do?* Harper tried to call her dad, but it went to voicemail.

"Mom, what are you doing? You're scaring me. Did something happen?" Harper moved closer to Abby

"Mom!!" Harper repeated but Abby seemed to be in some kind of half-conscious state, like a trance. Harper could tell that her mom heard her, because when she said mom, her shoulders relaxed from their erect state, but only for a moment.

"Mom, please answer us. Are you alright? I can't reach dad on his cell. He should be home soon. Should I call Uncle Tab? I hear police sirens in the distance. Did you call the police?"

On that last word, Alex touched Abby's shoulder. She spun around and looked right through both of her daughters. It was as if there was someone else behind her eyes. Alex grabbed Harper by the hand and ran into the living room. Just as they reached the front door, they heard the back door open and what sounded like a bat hitting something or maybe someone. All they could do was pray; *God help us*.

#

Just this morning Detective Hawkins solved the puzzle. It took many years and a lot of research, but he finally figured it out. He had to call in a few favors from his friends back at the Brookhaven Police Department. He also learned that there were some detectives inquiring about him the last few weeks. They knew where he lived and worked. He knew locating him wouldn't take long if they were any good at their jobs. He had only ventured back to Summit once or twice to watch that store the Stewarts went to. All along, he was sure that was the connection and now he had proof.

He wondered if Abby knew the truth about her family. He doubted it, since his original search only confirmed that her parents were Josephine, and Alcee Fontenot. With both of them gone, he couldn't find out what she was told and that was unfortunate. He didn't like to bring information as sensitive as this to anyone, but she had to know, so it would have to come from him.

Detective Hawkins had been following Abby waiting for the right time to try and approach her again. After their last encounter, he was more cautious. The walking stick was already affecting Abby, but he wasn't sure to what level. All the other people who were in possession of the stick had already gone over the edge by the time he got to them. He could only piece together what had happened from the person themselves and the people around them. The only bad thing was the person committing the crime could never recall what happened. They always described it as a blur or even a total blackout. And the people around them only saw bits and pieces from the murderers and often described their most recent behavior as odd and not normal. It was only when it was too late, that it all came together and was brought to his attention. He was not going to let that happen to Mrs. Stewart.

He followed her earlier that morning when she and Olivia went for a walk, but he never had an opportunity to talk to her. Then he followed her and her detail to Gattuso's and shopping after that. When she finally went home, her youngest daughter was there and not long after the other daughter came. So, he sat and waited for the right time to come.

It was almost dark when he noticed Abby slipping out the back door. It appeared she was going for a walk because she had that stick with her. He figured it was now or never, so he slipped into the woods and kept a safe distance. When he felt like the time was right, he grabbed her and tried to drag her into the woods. He needed to get her where he could have her undivided attention. He did surprise her and was able to stop her from screaming but then everything went crazy. The last thought he had before everything went black was, *It's later than I thought.*

#

Griff busted through the back door to find Abby standing there with a golf club ready to strike. She immediately came forward with all her force and struck him in the leg. He leaped forward and they both went down. They struggled for what seemed like forever and finally, he was able to pin her down.

Griff couldn't understand what the hell was happening. Just a few minutes ago, they drove up from Summit to find Abby beating the hell out of someone. There was blood everywhere and he thought it was Abby's. He leaped out of the car and knocked her to the ground, only then realizing she was the attacker. She didn't even recognize him and took off running towards the house.

Tab and Trey were right behind him and checked on the victim. It was Detective Hawkins, unconscious and full of blood, but thankfully, still breathing. They called for an ambulance and secured the scene. Griff ran after Abby only to find her still out of her mind and ready to attack anybody.

He was immediately worried about his daughters. Where were they and were they alright? Abby put up one hell of a fight, but she hurt her shoulder and dropped the golf club during the fall to the floor when she and Griff started wrestling. That slowed her down and once he had her secured, he yelled for the girls.

"Harper! Alex! Harper! Alex! Its dad, are you alright?" Griff yelled; panic stricken.

All of a sudden, Abby became completely calm. It was almost like a switch had turned, and while she still looked confused, that blank darkness in her eyes was gone. He let her go and ran into the other room looking for his children. He found them both crouched behind the sofa and ready to pounce.

"Oh my God, Dad!" Harper ran to him, and Alex followed.

Griff sighed with relief, "Are you girls alright? Moms alright. She's in the kitchen still dazed and confused, but she's alright. What happened here?"

Alex looked at Harper and they both shrugged their shoulders. Neither one really knew. Alex explained that she woke up and went to check on their mother, but she wasn't in bed. She searched the house, and then woke up Harper. A few minutes later, their mother burst through the back door and was out of her mind. After that, everything happened so fast. They didn't know what to do. They were afraid of what was outside, but also afraid of their mother.

Griff told them to stay put and went back to Abby. She was just lying there on the floor with a terrified look in her eyes. He took her in his arms and held her tight telling her everything would be okay. After a few moments, the girls came into the kitchen, and joined Griff in embracing their mother. He took a little comfort in knowing that his family was strong, and they would get through this.

Tab knocked on the open back door and walked in. He assessed the situation and it appeared everyone was alright.

"Griff, buddy is everyone alright in here?"

Griff looked up with terror in his eyes. *Define what alright means.* He was not sure how to answer that question, but knew Tab was asking about their physical well-being more than their emotional.

"I think Abby should go to the hospital. She took two nasty falls and I'd rather her get checked out. I know she hurt her shoulder but not sure if she has any other injuries."

"Alright man, I'll get them in here to get her." Tab walked down the street to where Trey was and told him to send the paramedics. After they loaded Abby into the ambulance Tab updated Griff on what he thought happened outside.

"It appeared Detective Hawkins attacked Abby and once again, she proved she was capable of defending herself. He's unconscious, but still alive. They just loaded him into the ambulance and are heading to the hospital. It looks like we have our man now, so you and your family should be safe. I'll leave you to your family and head to the hospital."

Griff thanked Tab and waited with Abby for the paramedics to come and get her. She had been completely quiet, but he could see in her eyes that she was scared. He just sat there silent, but his mind was unsteady with thoughts of the last few weeks. *What if Detective Hawkins dies? How would Abby be able to live with that?* Tab said he was unconscious, but hopefully he comes around so we can get some answers. *Once before, Abby said she thought the detective was trying to tell her something but what could that be? She didn't even know that man. And why not contact us and say what he had to say?* Tab tried to assure him that they were safe now, but he had an uncanny feeling that they were still not safe, not by a long shot. He just couldn't wrap his head around what the true threat could be. Evil. Definitely something evil, and it had hold of his wife. He shuddered at that thought and the thought that even Tab, who had always been by his side, wouldn't be able to help him with this one. All he could do was wait to get to the hospital and hopefully talk to the detective. He had a bad feeling that they went about this all wrong and that Detective Hawkins was not a threat, but in fact held the key to all of this.

Within an hour, they were in the hospital emergency room waiting to see a doctor. Abby's condition didn't appear to be life threatening, so they had to wait. They brought Detective Hawkins in earlier and rushed him to the back, but still no word on his condition. Tab had an officer stationed outside the doors they took him behind. He promised to update Griff as soon as he received any information.

Harper and Alex wanted to go to the hospital with Abby, but Griff talked them into staying at home. They were both a wreck and in need of some down time. They promised him they would stay at the house and stay together. Alex thought about going to her house, but decided she was in no shape to face Gabrielle. Her daughter was very perceptive and would immediately know something was wrong. Alex called Finn and filled him in on what was going on. He offered to come to the house, but they both agreed it would be too much for Gabrielle.

While they were waiting to be seen, Griff called Olivia to fill her in.

"I can be there in ten minutes."

"Liv, I just wanted to let you know what was going on. Abby appears to be alright physically, but she has been quiet since this happened. She still appears to be confused and maybe even in shock. I need you to contact her therapists first thing in the morning and fill her in. I think Abby is going to need some help with this one." Griff looked at his wife and felt helpless.

"Please tell her I love her and if she needs me for anything, I'm here. Griff I'm here for you too. Everything's going to be alright."

Griff hung up and went to sit next to Abby. She was really scaring him. He wanted to ask her how she was feeling. He wanted to know what she was thinking. He wanted to know exactly what the heck happened. Instead of all those questions, he simply put his arm around his wife, pulled her close to him and continued to wait to be seen.

CHAPTER 33

It was three days before the big Halloween Party, and everything was quiet. It had been about a week and half since Abby was released from the hospital. They had admitted her for observation and ran a few tests. She had a dislocated shoulder and a few bumps and bruises. They did a cat scan to make sure she didn't hit her head. It was midnight before she was in a room, and they gave her something to sleep. Griff stayed with her but was unable to get any sleep. The next morning, she woke up and had no recollection of the events from the night before. This concerned Griff, but at the same time he was glad she was back to normal. Well not normal but at least talking. She was very agitated and impatient with everyone. They released her that afternoon and said to follow up with her primary doctor.

When they got home, the girls and Olivia were there. She seemed happy to see them but didn't want to talk about anything except the upcoming Halloween Party. Griff thought about suggesting they cancel it but decided to let her make that decision

They all enjoyed casual conversation. Abby tried to participate but found it difficult to get out of her head.

Things keep popping in and out of her memory. She figured it was probably the effect of the sleeping medicine they gave her the night before. Those medications made her drowsy and disorientated. She was trying to determine what was a dream and what was real. She was not ready to discuss it with anyone, yet. *How can I make them understand when I'm not sure what happened myself?* She decided she needed some alone time to try to think through what had happened. She turned her attention to them and started discussing the preparations for the Halloween Party

It was crunch time before the party and everyone was running around crazy. They only had a few days to make everything come together. Normally, Abby would pull it all together, but Griff was concerned it might be too much for her. He had invited Olivia and the girls over for breakfast to offer support. He told Abby he wanted everyone to regroup and make sure they all knew what had to be done. Abby jumped right in and went over everything left to do.

"I have an appointment with my therapists tomorrow at 10am, but can we have lunch and finalize the plans for the party tomorrow?" Abby asked Olivia.

"Sure. I don't have any plans. How are you feeling?"

"Why is everyone asking me that? I'm fine, alright. Harper, Alex, Griff did you hear me, I'm fine! Stop grilling me!" Abby walked out of the kitchen and left them all standing there flabbergasted and wondering what that was all about.

#

Tab called Griff every day with an update on Detective Hawkins. He was still unconscious but was healing physically. While there was swelling around his brain, they didn't think he would have any permanent damage, just superficial wounds. It appeared he hit his head when they fell back and that's why he was still unconscious. They were keeping him sedated, giving him time to rest and were hoping for a full recovery. Abby still didn't know what she did, and they were not going to tell her right now. Her therapist was hoping to ease her memory back a little at a time.

#

Things were tense that night, so they all turned in early. Abby was still on edge, but she took her sleep medication and was out early. Harper stayed home, but Abby talked Alex into going home. She promised to be back in the morning as soon as she dropped Gabby off at school.

Lying in bed next to his sleeping wife, Griff began to pray. He didn't understand what was happening to his family, but he knew that whatever it was only God could help. For the longest time he felt like the detective was the threat, but not anymore. His wife's behavior was so disturbing and that couldn't be blamed on any human being; there had to have been some kind of outside influence or force. He couldn't quite explain it, but he could feel the danger. Normally, he wouldn't even consider thoughts like that, but things were way past normal. *The threat to this family is coming from within, but how and why?* He spent the rest of the night going over all the events leading them up to that point and only one thing stood out: a store. Everything began after they visited that store in Summit and even though he went back and unfortunately found no answers, he knew that was the connection. He couldn't leave Abby right now but as soon as he could, he would get to the bottom of it all.

#

Abby got up early the next morning but didn't feel like exercising. Truth be told, she could've slept in all morning long. She could handle all the crazy things that were happening lately, but what she couldn't stand, was being treated her like a weak child. She guessed it was her own fault because all they ever saw was her being laid back and positive about things. But they shouldn't confuse a positive outlook for weakness. She was a strong independent woman and could and would take care of herself and her family. *God help the person that tried to hurt them.*

She showered and dressed for her therapist's appointment. She felt fine and really didn't want to go, but Griff would pitch a fit if she cancelled. She was going to get it over with, then meet Olivia for lunch. They had a lot to do before the big party, which was coming up fast. She called Olivia on her way out the door.

"Good morning. My appointment is for 10:00am, so can we meet at 11:30am for lunch?"

"That's the plan." Olivia hung up, unsure what to expect. Abby was usually unpredictable, but always positive and optimistic. Lately her behavior was flat out unpredictable. She just hoped her therapists, could help her and they could get on with their normal, happy lives.

#

Abby showed up at her appointment early, as usual. She was a little apprehensive and didn't understand why. All they do was talk about things going on and even though a lot was going on she usually let Abby do most of the talking. For once, she wished someone would give her some answers or at least offer an opinion.

The nurse called her back. As she sat in the office waiting for the doctor, she began to feel aggravated that she was waiting so long. *Why are doctors always so late? Why should I have to wait on the doctor? Of course, they're busy, but so is everyone else.* Abby was getting more impatient as each minute passed. She went from feeling completely calm to out of control very quickly. Just as she was ready to walk out, in walked the Doctor.

"Good morning, Abby. How are you feeling today?"

"I've been better." She tried to calm down. The last thing she needed was for her doctor to think she was out of control. Then what would happen? She took a deep breath and used the techniques this very doctor taught her to use. Her annual Halloween party was happening soon, and she was not going to let anything interfere with it. She looked forward to it all year long.

This year it was going to be epic. Thanks to Griff and her girls the garage looked like the real laboratory from *Morgus The Magnificent* television show. It occurred to her that her mood lately identified with that theme, diabolical. She wondered, *Is that a good thing or a bad thing?* She chuckled a little before she realized the doctor was waiting for her to answer a question. She straightened up and asked her to repeat the question. The rest of the session went on uneventful, and Abby was careful to supply all the right answers.

"What do you remember about the night you ended up in the hospital?"

Abby was stunned momentarily, but quickly answered. "I remember everything. I thought someone was breaking into the house, so I grabbed a golf club and started swinging only to realize it was Griff. He tackled me to the ground, and I hurt my shoulder. He just wanted to make sure I was okay, so he insisted I go to the hospital" Abby stayed calm.

"Is that all? Nothing happened before that. What were you doing before that?" The doctor was studying Abby's face to see any sign that she might start to remember.

Abby again took a moment before she answered. "I was taking a nap. When I woke up the girls were napping on the sofa, so I went into the kitchen to get a drink of water. And as I said earlier, someone was at the back door, and I thought it was someone trying to break in. I was afraid for my life and my daughters were both there. I couldn't let anything happen to them." She rocked back and forth and started to sound upset. She could see her doctor believed everything she was saying, and that was just what she wanted. What she didn't say was that she remembered everything. She remembered having a bad dream and then when Harper tried to wake her, she attacked her own daughter. She remembered beating the hell out of that Detective that tried to pull her into the woods. They all think she didn't remember any of it, but she did.

She remembered how good it felt to beat that guy up. *He deserved every bit of it for coming after me.* Griff has been getting updates on his condition from Tab every day. He thought she wouldn't be able to handle the truth, so he never mentioned it. She herself has had updates on his condition all along. A friend of hers worked at the hospital and had been keeping her updated. Her last update was that he was still unconscious, but they were hopeful he would regain consciousness soon.

They all wanted to tip toe around her, so she was going to play along. She was not interested in talking about it anyway. *They have no idea how I feel and what I am capable of. They can't help me, nobody can.* She was sorry that she attacked Harper, but it's not like she hurt her. She woke up in time to realize what was happening. If they knew she remembered and wasn't upset about what she did, they would think something was wrong and insist she get more help. Maybe even have her committed and that was not happening. *I am not crazy. I am tired of being the nice one. Those days are over.*

She called Griff when she was walking out of her appointment. He kept her on a short string these days. She knew if she didn't check in, he'd go crazy. Besides, he would want to know how it went. She stopped for a second and thought, *This must be how Harper feels. Like a child who can't make a move without reporting in.* She made a mental note to give Harper more space. She told Griff all about her session and he sounded satisfied but disappointed. She guessed he was hoping she would get her memory back. They all were.

Next, she sent Olivia a text to let her know she was on her way. Abby knew she would also want to hear all about the session. At that point, Abby felt like she could really use a drink. And that's exactly what she did the minute they sat down for lunch.

"So, how did it go today?"

Abby took a breath, and thought, *Here we go again.* "It went fine. I keep telling all of you that I am fine. We went over the details of that night and that was it. I don't know what y'all expect from me. I know I've been on edge lately but come on. You know me and I'm not going to let this stuff get to me. Can we please focus on the party?"

"Absolutely, as long as you know I'm here if you need me. What's first up on today's agenda?"

"We need to get to the store and pick up the rest of the stuff we need to start cooking. Then get back to the house and start. This year we ordered a lot of the food instead of making it all because we are short of time. Griff and the girls are making sure everything else is done."

Moving on Olivia asked, "Did you get a head count on the guest list?"

Abby sounded excited and said, "Yes. There are only a few people who can't make it. Oh, and did I tell you, Harper invited Noah. I sure hope things go well for them; I know she really likes him. God knows the last one was all wrong for her. I'm glad he is out of the picture. She was so hurt just after the breakup; I could've killed Ted myself. Thankfully, she realized she wasn't in love with him."

"Oh." Olivia didn't know what to say. She had never heard Abby talk about wanting to kill Harpers ex-boyfriend before; that came out of nowhere. "Well good for her. Let's get started then. Time is ticking."

Abby was pleased with the RSVPs she got this year. They always had a good turnout, usually their same old friends and family. This year they extended the guest list to include some new friends and Harper and E. R's friends. And to have her children and grandchildren become a part of this meant the world to her. That was one thing she was looking forward to this year.

After lunch, Abby and Olivia headed over to the grocery store and picked up what they needed. They spent the rest of the day cooking and preparing food. As usual, they had the music on and were singing and laughing like old times. Abby always loved music. She often said she could feel it in her soul.

Griff walked into the kitchen and just watched his wife cook and cut up with her best friend. Maybe therapy helped her today. She seemed to be back to the old Abby. He walked back outside and felt like a weight was lifted off his shoulder and thought maybe everything would be alright.

CHAPTER 34

The day of the annual Halloween Party had finally arrived. Abby woke up early before everyone else. She had slept surprisingly well. She finally had everyone convinced that she was alright. Just because she had changed, didn't mean it was for the worst. She liked the way she felt these days. She felt in control of her life. She felt strong and confident. Sure, she was more aggressive, but so what. Maybe that was how she needed to be to take care of herself. Her new rule: *If you mess with her, she'll make sure it'd be the last time you got to do that. Just like Detective Hawkins.* Twice he attacked her but the second time she made sure it would be the last. He was just lucky Griff got there in time and caught her off guard. Otherwise, he would be dead.

She showered and headed downstairs to start the day. The weather was beautiful, with only a small chance of rain later. It would be perfect for a morning walk, but she decided to skip it today; too much to do. The rest of the day went by quickly and before she knew it, it was party time.

Griff, Harper, and Alex did an amazing job transforming the shed into a laboratory. They covered the walls with white visqueen and used old white sheets to cover the tables. They ripped them then splattered them with fake blood and dirt. They even set up a table to look like an operating table. They had things like skulls, beakers, forceps, funnels, and test tubes all over the place. Harper even made jello-shots in small syringes to serve to the guest. It reminded Abby of a haunted house; it was so realistic.

The guests began to arrive, and the DJ started playing music. Everything was perfect. Abby was Morgus the Magnificent, and Griff was Chopsley. They were both in the shed greeting their guest. Abby's favorite part of the whole party was trying to figure out who was who. Most of their guests came in mask. Only a few of them didn't participate, which was alright with her. Abby was amazed at just how many people thought she was Griff dressed as Morgus. Boy were they going to be surprised!

Abby spotted Harper talking to someone dressed like a Vampire with a small child dressed the same. It must be Alex, because she always liked to dress her whole family in the same theme, and always something scary. Harper herself was dressed as the Bride of Frankenstein. She looked great. She said Noah was coming as Frankenstein. This should be interesting because there are a lot of people here dressed like that. She guessed with the laboratory theme everyone had the same idea. In fact, Olivia was supposed to come as Frankenstein, but changed her mind. She wouldn't tell Abby her new idea and said she had to wait and see.

Harper saw Noah and ran to greet him. He was dressed as Frankenstein and wearing a mask, but Harper would know him anywhere. She was so happy to finally get to spend some time with him.

"Hey you. I'm so glad you're here." Harper smiled at him.

"How'd you know it was me? I noticed there are a lot of Frankenstein's here," he said laughing.

"What do you mean, I'd know you anywhere. Besides you're the best looking one here."

Noah met her eyes, "Right back at you. Hey, I didn't know you lived in this neighborhood. We were just here recently investigating an assault. My boss's best friend lives around here."

Before she could answer someone grabbed Harper from behind and spun her around.

All the person had to say was "Guess who" and she knew it was Henly. She was dressed like the character "Eleven" from "Stranger Things" and her date was dressed like the character "Mike." They both had mask on, but she was fairly sure that was Oliver with her.

"Henly! I love your costumes. I thought you were going to be something else."

Henly smiled with pride that her best friend approved of her costume choice. "I wanted to surprise you. I know you've been so worried about your mom, and I wanted to cheer you up. How'd I do?" She did a spin and proceeded to curtsy.

Harper smiled back and hugged her. "You did great." Turning to Henly's date, Harper asked, "Who might this be?" Again, she figured it was Oliver, but you never know. She wouldn't want to make that mistake.

"You remember Oliver from Biloxi. I know I told you that he didn't think he would be in town for the party, but he found out today he would be."

The four of them hung around talking and laughing for a while. Some of their other friends arrived and joined them. After a while Harper turned to Noah and said, "Come on and meet my parents. Well my father any way. You met my mother at the restaurant a while back."

She spotted her mother first, so they went up to say hi. Abby was so glad to see him there. He seemed to make her daughter happy. The three of them looked around for Griff. Harper spotted him first and ran over to grab him.

"Hey Dad, I want you to come and meet Noah."

They headed back to where she left them. It took a few minutes because it was getting so crowded now. Just as they walked up, another couple walked up. They were dressed up as Dr. Jekyll and Mr. Hyde and Harper knew exactly who they were.

She kissed Dr. Jekyll on the cheek and whispered, "Hello Uncle Tab."

"Uncle Tab? He's your uncle?" Noah said looking confused.

"Not really but yes. He's my dad's best friend."

Before she could say anymore, her dad and uncle Tab said at the same time, "Trey is that you?"

Noah looked confused then started to put two and two together. "Griff is your dad? I can't believe this. Mr. Tab is my boss Harper. I've been working with them on a case the last few weeks. I had no idea Griff was your dad."

Now it was Harpers turn to look confused. "But they called you Trey."

"That's my nickname my family calls me. Noah Doucet III, Trey. Tab and your father were old college buddies of my dad. He asked Tab to give me an opportunity to work with him for a while. Oh my God! I didn't realize all of this was happening to your family. Abby's your mom! I really didn't remember your mom's name. Harper, I am so sorry. Now I understand why you've been so unavailable lately."

Everyone stood around catching up and laughing about the chances of that happening. E.R. finally showed up with his friends to make the night complete. Abby stood back and glowed with joy because all was well with her family. That was until she saw him slip into the back door.

CHAPTER 35

He woke up in an unfamiliar room in an unfamiliar place. His vision was blurred, and he had a splitting headache. *Where am I? What the heck happened? How long was I out?* He attempted to get up but became dizzy and had to lie back down.

Think! Think! He closed his eyes. The last thing he remembered was following Mrs. Stewart. His eyes flew open. *Mrs. Stewart! I need to warn her.* He tried again to get out of bed but this time a nurse came in and stopped him.

"Mr. Hawkins, do you know where you are?"

The hospital, that's where he was, the hospital, now he remembered. He tried to warn Mrs. Stewart again and she attacked him, again. If it wouldn't have been for her husband showing up, he might be dead. He laid back down to satisfy the nurse and to catch his breath.

"How long have I been here? What day is it?"

The nurse checked all his IVs to make sure he didn't mess anything up. "Almost two weeks. Today is October 28th Mr. Hawkins. Can you tell me the year?"

"Of course I can, it's 2017. My name is Clay Hawkins. I'm a retired detective from the Brookhaven Police Department. Now can you get the doctor because I have to get out of here?"

He sat back and tried to stay calm. *Was it too late? Did she already go off the deep end?* He really hoped not. As he lay there waiting for the doctor, he went over the story in his head that he needed to make sure Mrs. Stewart knew. He wondered if Mrs. Stewart even knew that Josephine Moreau Fontenot and Alcee Fontenot were not really her parents but in fact her aunt and uncle. And that her real parents were Claude, Josephine's brother, and his wife Marie Moreau. Back in 1962, her father Claude killed her mother Marie and then himself leaving Abby an orphan. Her aunt Josephine took her and moved to New Orleans to raise her. *Is it possible she doesn't know?*

Mrs. Stewart might know some of it, but probably doesn't know that whole mess started in 1891 with her Great, Great, Grandfather, who left his first wife after a year of marriage, for her sister. Viola Rochon, his first wife cursed them both and their children. The Rochon sisters were originally from New Orleans and after the divorce Viola simply disappeared, but her curse lived on.

Once Detective Hawkins came upon the information about Mrs. Stewarts past, everything started coming together. All of his questions were answered. All of the bizarre murders he had investigated were connected one way or another.

The first one back in 1967 was an old man named Clarence Baptiste, Abby's Great Grandfather's brother. He apparently went crazy and attacked and beat to death two people. Next in 1977, they never did solve that murder, because they had no murder weapon and no suspect. But oddly enough the victim was the granddaughter of Mary Baptiste Collins, Abby's Great Grandfather's sister. The 1987 case had him baffled. It occurred in New Orleans and even though he knew it was connected to the other ones, he didn't know how until now. The woman was Roberta Baptiste Shanely and again related to Mrs. Stewart. She was Mrs. Stewart's Grandmother Simone Baptiste Moreau's sister.

As he continued running all the details over in his mind, he became agitated. His heart rate rose, and his breath quickened. He tried to stop thinking about it for a moment. It was all so crazy; how would he make her see the danger she was in?

It didn't take long for his mind to go to the next case. In 1997, Morton McCalister, grandson of Samuel Baptiste, killed one person and severely beat another. Samuel was also related to Mrs. Stewart's Grandmother, Simone's sister. Finally, in 2007, he knew they were all related, when in McComb, Mississippi a woman named Adeline Baptiste beat to death a man and was found wondering around outside by her neighbors, another relative of Mrs. Stewart's Great, Grandfather, Claude. She was the granddaughter of his brother Henry.

So, there it was. A curse that started back in 1891 was still going on today. He knew it sounded crazy, heck he didn't believe it for the longest time. This was the kind of thing you see in movies. It was not until he finally realized that Mrs. Stewart was related to all those people, that he started to believe in the curse. That sealed it. And the one thing they all had in common was that old walking stick. And he confirmed recently that his hunch was right all along, they all got it from the same store in Summit.

He closed his eyes and tried to relax. He was haunted by the look in Mrs. Stewart's eyes the last time he tried to warn her. She was definitely showing the same behavior as the others, but was it too late? Doctor or no doctor, he needed to get out of that hospital bed.

Everything was going so well at the party. Abby was having a great time with her guest. Olivia and Jack showed up as "The Six Million Dollar Man" and "The Bionic Woman". Olivia looked amazing in her outfit but that wasn't surprising, she was always in great shape. Others came as "Mulder" and "Scully" from "X-Files." Her guest came up with costumes she never even thought of that went with the theme of a Laboratory. And, as she thought earlier, the garage looked awesome. Harper used the internet to find pictures to recreate the laboratory they used for the *Morgus the Magnificent* show. She even managed to scrounge up an old wall telephone that Morgus so often used. She recreated the skull with the spiral wires going into the box he used. She really did a great job, and everyone seemed to be enjoying themselves. The rest of the house was decorated in a mixture of fall colors and Halloween décor. That was what Abby loved about Halloween. Some people thought it was silly to dress up, but not her, and apparently not most of their friends.

She was worried about the food because this year they had a lot of it catered. They cooked what they could and ordered the rest. She made her rounds and was happy to see that everyone was enjoying the food, the home cooked and the catering. That might just be the new tradition.

Abby enjoyed cooking, but it does get to be stressful so if it worked well this year that was the way they would do it the following years. Who knows, next year Harper might help with the cooking too. Alex never did like to cook, so she couldn't count on her help. Abby was simply happy to have both of her girls there and having a good time.

It was all going smoothly, that was until he showed up. Why couldn't he just leave them alone? At first, she wasn't sure it was him. It was dark and there were so many people everywhere wearing costumes. When she recognized him, he was entering the house and turned to look back.

She tried to go after him right away, but it took a while; so many of her guests stopped her along the way. By the time she got to the back door, he was nowhere to be found. She searched the rooms knowing he had to be there but came up empty. She wanted to sit by the back door and wait until he surfaced again but someone was asking for more plates. He was here for a reason, and she knew he was going to show up again soon. She went after the plates but was mindful that danger was in her house, and she was going to end it once and for all tonight.

Abby tried to enjoy herself as much as she could while she waited. She was still not used to the way her feelings changed so easily. One moment she felt completely at peace and the next she wanted to hurt someone. She watched Harper and Noah dance and hoped things would work out for them. She didn't know much about him, but her husband spoke highly of him. *How did they not realize Trey was Noah?* It made her chuckle to think that slipped by all of them, even Tab. *How good of a detective is he?* She thought back to the events leading up to this night and couldn't help blaming him for the way things turned out. If he would have done his job right and found the detective, things would have turned out differently. But, as it turned out, she had to take matters into her own hands and put an end to it herself. Well not completely ended. She thought she ended it by putting Detective Hawkins in the hospital.

Still aware that danger lurked in her house she went in to check again. She found it difficult to engage in small talk with her friends while she knew the intruder was somewhere watching them. Coming up empty again she walked back outside. Someone grabbed her from behind and for a moment her heart stopped. Thankfully, it was Griff pushing her towards the dance floor. She could tell he'd had a few drinks and was on top of the world. She relaxed as much as she could and let him lead her there. She would rather not dance, but if she let on that something was wrong, he'd think she was being paranoid.

It was not going unnoticed that he thought something was wrong with her. Heck, she knew that she had changed lately, but that didn't mean something was wrong. *Maybe this was how I want to feel.* She had noticed that over the past few weeks her thoughts seemed to have become reality in some cases. Everyone had ill thoughts about someone at one time or another. It was not like she had acted on them. She couldn't explain it, but situations just seemed to go the way she thought they should. She got an unusual feeling when each event happened. If that made her a bad person, then so be it.

#

He couldn't believe that he was able to slip into the Stewarts Halloween party that easily. He wasn't sure if he should have come, but he had to talk to her. He wished she would just give him five minutes to explain, he knew she'd feel differently. He had tried several times before and failed. He had to make her see he was not the bad guy she thought he was.

He thought she saw him when he first arrived. He ran into the back door and out the front. He decided to lay low for a while until he was sure it was safe to go in and try again. She would never listen to him if he were to just walk up to her, so he had to catch her off guard. He was hoping, towards the end of the night, he could get her alone and finally make her see the truth. He had been watching her dance and enjoying the evening. From where he was hiding, he could see almost everyone at the party. All he could do was wait for his chance to make things right again.

#

It was late in the night before Abby saw him again. He was in the laundry room standing right in the back door looking around for her, she knew it. Most of her guests were outside in the garage now. She quickly went around to the front door and entered the house. Her heart was beating fast, and her hands were sweating as she went to find her walking stick. She could feel the anger building up inside of her. She embraced the feeling rather than fight it. She found comfort in it that she didn't quite understand, but also didn't care. For a while, she was confused and scared of the way she was feeling. And her mind was telling her that the Old lady held the key to all of this. But by now, things were different. She didn't need or want answers. It felt like she was slipping into some kind of darkness, and she welcomed it.

She came up behind him and hit him in the back of the head with her walking stick. He fell to the floor, unconscious and she acted quickly. She tied his hands, found some tape on one of the shelves above the dryer, and put it over his mouth. Then, she grabbed his Halloween mask, and covered his face. With a strength she didn't recognize, but welcomed, she dragged him through the house, and out the front door. She didn't want anyone to see her or to stop her. He sealed his own fate when he came there tonight.

In the darkness of the night, she dragged him into the woods just across the street from their house, and at that moment, he regained consciousness. She could hear him trying to mumble under the tape and the mask. She removed the mask from his head and just stared at him. She could see the terror in his eyes. She could feel the fear in him. Instead of feeling sorry for him, it fueled her, and she lifted the stick to end it all. She could almost feel the satisfaction of protecting her family. She would not allow anyone to come close to hurting them ever again, especially Harper.

Out of nowhere, someone grabbed the end of the stick. It happened so quickly that Abby stood still, confused for a moment. But only for a moment, because she turned to see Detective Hawkins standing behind her with her walking stick in his hand. He tackled her to the ground and threw the stick as far from Abby as he could. She was fighting him as hard as she could to get back to her victim. She was not going to let Ted near Harper ever again. He hurt her daughter and it took a while for her to find someone new. He had no business showing up here, not now, not ever. He kept mumbling about making Harper see he was not the bad guy. She reached to try to grab the stick, but it was too far away.

Detective Hawkins began to yell, hoping someone would hear him. He was going to need help if he was going to stop Mrs. Stewart. He could see the evil that dwelled. He was weak, but he was not giving up. She had to listen to him. He started rattling off all the things he wanted her to hear, to understand, but she was too far gone to listen.

She was getting the best of him, and he was afraid she was going to win, and at the last moment Griff showed up, with Tab by his side. Tab grabbed the detective, just as Griff tackled his wife. She put up a fight for a while, but he finally subdued her. When Griff pulled back to look at his wife's face, he saw that she was just staring into the darkness, with a numb look on her face. Tab untied Ted's hands and took the tape off of his mouth. He made sure he wasn't hurt other than the bump on the back of his head and, thankfully, it wasn't bleeding. He called for an ambulance anyway. It was probably best that someone take a look at him.

Griff picked up his wife and carried her into the house. After cuffing Detective Hawkins, Tab escorted him inside instead of taking him into the station. It was time to get answers and he knew Griff and Abby would want to hear everything. The detective looked awful and could barely stand up on his own. It was a miracle this guy was even alive after the beating he took. Tab wondered if they released him from the hospital or if he just left on his own. There was a detail cop stationed outside his room since he had been admitted. *How did he manage to give them the slip?* He had a million questions, but number one on the list was, *What did he want with Abby?*

Detective Hawkins took what seemed like forever to explain everything to them and when he was finished, they all sat there in silence trying to absorb what he said. He knew that it was a lot to take in and exceedingly difficult to follow.

"Bottom line", he continued, "This was all part of a curse that started a long time ago with Mrs. Stewarts Great, Great, Grandfather and Grandmother. Your family history is filled with tragedy and death. It wasn't until I found out an old lady gave the stick to Abby that I figured out how the stick was just showing up. It sounds bizarre but I think that old lady is Viola Rochon herself. I don't know how yet but I hope to find out."

Detective Hawkins sat back for a moment before he went on. "There was one more thing. I often wondered what my connection was to these cases and now I finally know. Abby's Grandmother Simone killed one of her own daughters and went into a mental institution. Her grandfather remarried a woman named Cecelia Hawkins, a young widow with a child. Cecelia was my mother."

He went on, "I don't know what's going to happen now. I know we have to get that walking stick as far away from Mrs. Stewart as possible. I tried to get it from her house when they went to Biloxi, but her daughter showed up and almost caught me. I had to run because I knew they wouldn't believe me. I only pray that she can find her way back from this darkness now. We need to go find the stick and destroy it and finally end the curse." Detective Hawkins looked at Tab and pleaded "Please believe me! It's the only way."

Everyone was sitting around speechless for several minutes. Finally, Tab and the detective went outside after the stick and Griff comforted Abby. She was still quiet but seemed to be coming out of it slowly. He was not sure how much she understood about what Detective Hawkins said. He was not even sure how much he understood. It was all a lot to comprehend. He didn't care about any of that right now. All he cared about was making sure his wife was safe and he would deal with the rest later.

They sat for a while longer, and then he heard her mumble something. Her voice was shallow and difficult to understand. He leaned in close and tried to listen.

All she said was "I can't believe I'm adopted. What the heck?"

And with that he knew she was on her way back to being the Abby he knew and loved. He finally saw a little light in the darkness, and they owe it all to the one person they thought was the threat, Detective Clay Hawkins.

CHAPTER 37

Detective Hawkins knew leaving the stick outside in the woods was a risk, but he didn't realize it would be gone that fast. By the time he and Tab went to look for the stick, it was gone. He only hoped that Mrs. Stewart would be alright. Usually it was too late to save them, but in her case, he stopped her from hurting that young man. And thanks to Mrs. Stewart, he now knew who he was looking for.

He knew Tab believed he was telling the truth even though he didn't understand it. Tab let Detective Hawkins go to try and track down the stick. If there was a chance this could affect someone else, he had to try to stop it and Tab agreed.

He knew exactly where to start looking. First thing in the morning he was headed to track down an "Old lady" in Summit, at a little store called Second Chances. That's exactly what he hoped he gave to Mrs. Stewart; a second chance.

ABOUT THE AUTHOR

D. M. Bourgeois was born in New Orleans and now resides in Crown Point, Louisiana with her husband Glenn. She received a B.A from Nicholls State University in Thibodaux, Louisiana, where she graduated Cum Laude in Interdisciplinary Studies with a minor in English and Humanities. She believes that her life is blessed, and aside from being a mother and grandmother, becoming an author is one of her greatest joys. She loves to read and is a member of several book clubs. She enjoys listening to music and spending time with family and friends.

For more information you can visit D. M. Bourgeois @
dmbourgeois61@gmail.com
Facebook.com/ D.M. Bourgeois